KIARA FIGHTS BACK

THE SPYGLASS SISTERHOOD #3

KIARA FIGHTS BACK

Marilyn Kaye

HOLIDAY HOUSE • NEW YORK

Printed and bound in February 2022 at Maple Press, York, PA, USA.
www.holidayhouse.com
First Edition
1 3 5 7 9 10 8 6 4 2

Library of Congress Cataloging-in-Publication Data

Names: Kaye, Marilyn, author.
Title: Kiara fights back / by Marilyn Kaye.
Description: First edition. | New York : Holiday House, [2022] | Series: The
spyglass sisterhood ; 3 | Audience: Ages 8-12. | Audience: Grades 4-6. |
Summary: When a classmate is being bullied online, Kiara and her friends
use their magical spyglass to find out who is behind the online posts and
bring the bully to justice.
Identifiers: LCCN 2021048947 (print) | LCCN 2021048948 (ebook) |
ISBN 9780823446117 (hardcover) | ISBN 9780823450312 (ebook)
Subjects: CYAC: Magic—Fiction. | Telescopes—Fiction. | Bullying—Fiction. |
Friendship—Fiction. | African Americans—Fiction. | LCGFT: Novels.
Classification: LCC PZ7.K2127 Ki 2022 (print) | LCC PZ7.K2127 (ebook) |
DDC [Fic]—dc23
LC record available at https://lccn.loc.gov/2021048947
LC ebook record available at https://lccn.loc.gov/2021048948

ISBN: 978-0-8234-4611-7 (hardcover)

For Lara Clerc, my goddaughter,
who knows all about courtrooms

one

MY FRIEND ELLIE MARKS SAYS I HAVE TO introduce myself before I start telling this story. My name is Kiara Douglas, and I will begin by saying to you all, "Greetings and salutations."

Six years ago, when I was in the first grade, my father read *Charlotte's Web* to me. If you don't know this book, it's by E. B. White, and it's about the friendship between a spider named Charlotte and a pig named Wilbur. When Charlotte first meets Wilbur, she says "Salutations!" Wilbur doesn't know what that means, and she tells him it's a fancy way of saying "Greetings."

I really liked that word, *salutations*. I added *greetings* in case the people I spoke to were like Wilbur and didn't know what *salutations* meant. So I began saying "Greetings and salutations" to the other kids in my classroom.

They laughed at me. The teacher told them to stop, so they did, but I saw some of them cover their mouths, and I'm sure they were giggling. It annoyed me that they couldn't appreciate my vocabulary.

I didn't have any friends in the first grade. Or in the second, third, fourth, or fifth. Then we moved to Lakeside and I began to attend East Lakeside Middle School. I didn't have any friends in the sixth grade there either. But now, in the seventh grade, I have friends—three of them. I'll tell you more about them later. But first I have to finish telling you about myself.

I've just turned thirteen years old. I'm Black, and my skin is brown. I wear my hair in cornrows, which are tight braids. I like this style because it's very neat and my hair doesn't get in my face. And also because my aunt braids it for me and I like to visit her.

I live with my father in a big apartment in a very

nice building. It has three bedrooms even though there are only two of us. My father uses the third bedroom as a study. His name is Edward James Douglas, PhD, and he's a professor of history at Bascomb College here in Lakeside. I don't have a mother. Well, I *did* have a mother, of course, who gave birth to me. Her name was Caroline Douglas, but she died in an accident when I was only two years old so I don't remember her. I've seen pictures of her, and she was pretty. My aunt Molly says I look like her, but I don't think so. Aunt Molly is my father's sister. She lives in Lakeside too, she's a hairdresser, and as I just told you, she's the one who designed my braids. I go to her regularly for upkeep, as she calls it.

My father works a lot. He teaches classes at the college, and when he's not teaching, he's at the library or in his study doing research for a book he's writing. He even works sometimes on weekends. But we always have breakfast together, and usually dinner too. There's a nice lady, Ms. Cavendish, who comes in every weekday to do housework and prepare dinners for us.

Every Wednesday, at nine o'clock in the evening, my father and I watch our favorite TV show together. It's called *Courthouse Chronicles,* and each week there's a different story about a crime and a trial.

Sometimes we take sides, prosecution or defense, and we discuss it afterward. And sometimes, when we're just talking together, we find excuses to use phrases they use a lot on the show, like when the accused person says "I wasn't even there" or the prosecuting attorney says "We gotta nail this guy."

What else can I say about myself? I'm a good student, especially in math and science, and I've already mentioned my vocabulary, which is bigger than what most kids my age have. I don't belong to any clubs at school and I don't play on any teams. I prefer to do things by myself, so I never really minded not having friends. Sometimes I wondered if that was normal. There have always been other kids in my classes who didn't have many friends, but most of them *wanted* to have friends. I didn't.

My father told me it was okay not to have friends. He said *he* didn't have friends and he was just fine. When I pointed out the people he knew at the college, he said they were his "colleagues," and perfectly nice, but not what he'd call friends. And he likes Aunt Molly, of course, but she's family, so I guess she doesn't count as a friend.

But like I said, I have friends now—Ellie, Alyssa, and Rachel. My father knows about them, and he met them once. We usually spend our time together at Ellie's, because she has the spyglass.

That's how we got to know each other, because of the spyglass. It's in this little room called a turret at the top of Ellie's house, and it has some very unusual qualities. I've never believed in magic before, but I think I have to say that this spyglass is magical. When you look through it, sometimes you just see Lakeside. But other times, you see things that aren't really there. But they always *mean* something.

One day, just two and a half months ago, Ellie looked through the spyglass and saw Alyssa flying over the town on a broomstick. When she got to know Alyssa, she found out that some people call Alyssa a witch because of the way she dresses. Alyssa's half Asian, with long, straight black hair, and she always wears black clothes, black nail polish, and black stuff around her eyes. Also, dangling earrings that look like miniature skulls. Her mother comes from India, so her skin is brown, but lighter than mine. She's tall and slender, and she doesn't smile much.

Alyssa sometimes says she actually wishes she could be a fairy-tale witch so she could put curses on people she doesn't like. Which are most people, frequently including her own family.

Ellie and Alyssa became friends, and then, one day, they looked in the spyglass and saw Rachel. She was walking with one of her mothers. Suddenly, as Ellie and Alyssa were watching her, Rachel turned into a small child, like about five years old, and she was holding her mother's hand. Ellie and Alyssa got to know her and found out that Rachel's parents are very protective. They never leave her alone and they don't like her to go places without them. Rachel said they treat her as if she was a little kid and so sometimes she feels like one.

That's when they figured it out—what the spyglass was showing them. They were seeing things that people felt, maybe what they were afraid of, or maybe what they wished for. When they saw me, I was playing in the park with make-believe animals. It took them a while to figure out why.

When we moved here to Lakeside, my father gave me my very own laptop computer, and I started playing games on it. My favorite was *The Amazing Maze,* a game where you become an animal and compete with other animals to get through a maze. I was playing with people I didn't know, who I never saw, and who could have lived anywhere in the world as long as they had internet.

I know that some parents don't like their kids to play online games, but my father is okay with it as long as the games aren't violent. He even said that maybe online friends were better for me than real-life friends. Now that I actually have real-life friends, I think he's a little nervous. He doesn't know them very well, so he can't know how nice they are.

But nobody's perfect, right? Not me, not my friends. I guess I should tell you what they look like and act like so you can imagine them in your mind. First of all, I'd better warn you—Aunt Molly says I can be brutally honest, and that's not always a good thing, she says. But I'm going to try to be accurate, so here goes.

Ellie is taller than me, but not as tall as Alyssa. I guess she'd be called average. She's not skinny like me, but she's not fat either. She is white and has brown hair, brown eyes, and a medium complexion with some freckles. She always says she's ordinary-looking, but I think she's kind of pretty. She's friendly, but she can be a little bossy.

I've already told you what Alyssa looks like. As for her personality, she isn't very friendly and she rolls her eyes a lot. Sometimes she makes jokes that I don't get. Ellie says she's just being sarcastic and that I shouldn't take everything so literally. But what other way is there? Personally, I think people should just say what they mean.

Rachel is shorter than the rest of us and she thinks she's fat but she's not, she's just sort of round, and personally, I think she's the prettiest of us. She has long curly blond hair that gets frizzy sometimes. Her skin is seriously white, and when she's embarrassed she turns pink, or even red. She's usually shy, and sometimes she can act kind of wimpy and nervous, but she's improving—she finally convinced her parents she doesn't have to be walked to and from school and she can do more on her own. And just last month, she won a seventh-grade election to be the class representative, so I guess she's not so shy anymore.

I know a little about their histories, like why Ellie's family moved here to Lakeside. Back in her hometown, Brookdale, her parents were trying to raise money for a homeless shelter, and a lot of people didn't want that. Those people ostracized the whole Marks family, and they didn't want to live there anymore.

Alyssa has a mother who's a famous surgeon, a stepfather who's a major architect, a stepbrother who's a big deal in high school, a stepsister who's training to be an Olympic figure skater, and a little brother who's an actor. So to stand out in this important family, she rebelled, went gloomy and hostile, and started dressing goth style.

Before Rachel was born, she had a sister who was killed by a car while crossing a street alone when she was ten. This was why her two mothers became so overprotective of her and were afraid of letting her out of their sight.

They don't know much about *my* history. And I'd like to keep it that way.

We're different, but we have one big thing in common—none of us fit into any of the cliques at East Lakeside Middle School. We're not on any sports teams like the athletes. We're all smart, but not all-the-time straight-A types like the brains. We're not very artsy like the drama kids and chorus members. And we are most definitely not eligible to belong to the popular crowd.

These are the ones we particularly don't like. Ellie says she was a member of the popular crowd back at her old school, and I can believe that. She looks like them, she dresses like them, and she has a lot of confidence. But those friends turned on her and treated her very badly, so after her family moved to Lakeside, she didn't want to have anything to do with the popular crowd here.

We never do what those kids do. We don't join school clubs or try out for cheerleading or volunteer for committees. And we don't do social media. No Instagram, no Snapchat, no YouTube, no TikTok or whatever new app happens to be available. Of course, since you have to be thirteen to use social media and a lot of seventh graders are only twelve, they're not supposed to be on these things, but they just lie about their ages and join anyway. I'm actually thirteen now, but I'm still not interested in social media. Those popular kids, they're *addicted* to that stuff. You see them in the halls between classes, practically glued to their phone screens.

We are not like them, and we don't want to have anything to do with them. We call them *the others*. Though Ellie *does* make an exception for a popular boy named Mike, because he doesn't act superior like the others and he isn't mean. Personally, I think Ellie wants him to be her boyfriend. Maybe he already is.

We *do* send each other text messages. Ellie finally got her first smartphone last month, so now we can all have a text group instead of sending separate texts to each one of us. We call ourselves the

Spyglass Sisterhood, and that's the name of our text messaging group. I don't really feel like Ellie, Alyssa, and Rachel are my sisters. But since I've never had a sister, I'm not sure what that would feel like.

I guess that's enough about me and them for now, and I can start telling a story about us.

two

I WOKE UP ON A CERTAIN TUESDAY MORNING
in April and I knew there was something special
about that day, but I couldn't remember what it was.
I got up and went into my usual routine. I went to
the bathroom, washed my face, brushed my teeth,
made my bed. I was putting on my jeans and a
T-shirt when it finally hit me why this day was different from the usual school day.

I opened a dresser drawer and began going
through the clothes. Finally, I found the I ♥ NY T-shirt
that my father brought back for me when he went to

a conference there. I'd never worn it before because I was afraid that if I did, people might ask me something about New York, and I wouldn't be able to answer them because I've never been there. So the T-shirt was nice and clean and not even wrinkled. I took off the top I was wearing and put it on.

Dad was already at the breakfast table in the kitchen when I walked in. He looked at me with interest.

"You're wearing that to school?"

"It's Special T-shirt Day," I told him as I poured some cereal into a bowl. "It's the only day when we're allowed to wear T-shirts like this."

He cocked his head to one side. "You mean, T-shirts about New York?"

"*No.* T-shirts with words. We're not allowed to wear T-shirts with words because they might bother someone. Some kids, mostly boys, used to wear T-shirts with the names of their favorite teams. But then, last month, some of them got into a big loud argument in the cafeteria over whose team was best and it turned into a real fight. So the principal decided we couldn't wear T-shirts like that anymore. And even for today, he announced on the intercom that we couldn't wear T-shirts with words that could offend anyone."

Dad nodded. "But what if someone doesn't like New York? You could offend that person with your shirt."

I didn't respond, I just gave him a look and added milk to my cereal.

"That was a joke," Dad said.

"I know," I replied.

"Then why aren't you laughing?"

"Because it wasn't funny."

He sighed. "But you know, Kiara, it's nice to let people know you appreciate their jokes, even if they're not very funny. I mean, you could at least *smile*."

I started eating so I wouldn't have to speak. Sometimes it bothers me when he tells me how to behave with people. This is something he's said I have to work on. I just don't get it. It isn't like I want to hurt people's feelings. But if something isn't funny, why should I laugh? This doesn't make sense to me. Still, Dad is a very smart person and he knows me better than anyone, so I figured he was probably right. I made a mental note to myself. *Laugh—or just smile—when people tell jokes*. Even if they weren't funny. It wasn't going to be easy.

"Are you coming straight home from school today?" he asked.

"I'll probably go to Ellie's," I told him.

"You spend a lot of time at her house," he commented. "What do you kids do there?"

I shrugged. "Just hang out." I hated to lie to him, but I told myself it wasn't really a lie. *Hanging out* means being with friends. I just couldn't tell him what we did while we were hanging out.

The spyglass is a secret, and the sisterhood is sworn to protect it. Even Ellie's parents don't know about it. They know the telescope is *there,* of course. But they don't know what it can do.

"You know, you could invite your friends to hang out *here* sometimes," Dad suggested.

I nodded. "Okay." But it isn't very likely. This apartment is nice. Alyssa and Rachel live in nice places too, and we never go there either. Only Ellie has the spyglass.

We left together. Dad offered me a lift to school, which he always does, even though it isn't on his way. Bascomb College is in the opposite direction from East Lakeside Middle School. If it's very cold or raining or snowing, or if I'm just feeling lazy, I take him up on his offer. But it was nice out today, and warm for April, so I told him I'd walk.

We said goodbye, but we didn't kiss or hug. I'm not a huggy-kissy kind of person, and my father respects that.

When I arrived at East Lakeside, I looked around at the other kids going into the school. I immediately noted with approval that my T-shirt fit right in. Not that I particularly *wanted* to fit in, I just didn't want to stand out. I spotted an I ♥ SAN FRANCISCO, an I ♥ CHICAGO, and an I ♥ LONDON. I wondered if those kids had actually been to those places or if their parents brought the T-shirts home as souvenirs. But I didn't ask them. I don't really talk much to many kids at school. Just my three friends.

In homeroom, some classmates had T-shirts about the environment. The boy who sat next to me, Kent O'Malley, wore a SAVE THE PLANET T-shirt , and Jim Berger's T-shirt said HUG A TREE. Emily Baron's T-shirt had a picture of Emily herself and her baby sister on it. Some of the T-shirts were supposed to be funny, like the one that said I EAT CAKE EVERY DAY BECAUSE IT'S SOMEBODY'S BIRTHDAY SOMEWHERE. I didn't laugh, though. It wasn't *that* funny.

By the time I got to English class later in the morning, I felt like I'd seen every T-shirt in the universe. English is not my favorite class. I don't like the kind of books we have to read very much. For a while, we were reading poetry, and I didn't like that at all. There was all this talk about "inner meaning" and symbolism. Ms. Gonzalez said we were supposed to interpret what poems really meant. Why couldn't these poets just *say* what they mean? Why did readers have to figure it out?

When I read, I want books about real life, like history or biography. The only stories I like a lot are science fiction. But English is the only class where my friends and I are together, so that makes it okay. I had to go to the restroom before I went there that day, though, so I didn't have time to talk to them before the bell rang.

Some of the teachers were wearing T-shirts too, and Ms. Gonzalez was one of them. Hers had a picture of a book with the words I'D RATHER BE READING.

"We've been discussing plays," she reminded us, "and this week, you've read *The Crucible* by Arthur Miller."

A couple of kids in the back groaned. Ms. Gonzalez gave them one of her looks, and they stopped.

I couldn't really blame those kids for groaning about *The Crucible*. There were a lot of mean people in it, and they talked in old-fashioned English. I didn't much like it either.

But I would never have made noises like those kids in the back of the room. I've been learning that sometimes you shouldn't respond exactly the way you feel. It isn't polite and you could hurt someone's feelings.

"How would you describe this play?" Ms. Gonzalez asked. "What was it about?"

There was a time when I used to bring my tablet to school. If I wasn't interested in the class, I'd hold the tablet under my desk and play games. But Ms. Gonzalez caught me one day, and I almost got into real trouble, so I don't do it anymore. With nothing else to do, I have to listen while classmates raise their hands and offer their ideas when they're called on.

I was surprised to see Rachel raise her hand. Rachel likes English class a lot, but she doesn't speak up unless she's called on. That's like me, but for a different reason. Rachel is just shy, and I'm sure she doesn't volunteer anything in her other classes either. I only volunteer when I'm positively certain of an answer, which can happen frequently in pre-algebra. Or if I'm very interested in something and I know a lot about it, which has never happened in this class.

Ms. Gonzalez looked particularly pleased to see Rachel's hand up. She would probably have turned cartwheels if I ever raised my hand.

"Yes, Rachel?"

"Injustice?" Rachel offered.

Ms. Gonzalez nodded. "Absolutely." She noticed another hand. "Noah?"

"It's about a bunch of weird people doing crazy stuff," he said.

Ms. Gonzalez smiled. "They may seem weird to us, and their actions might be called unusual nowadays. But keep in mind that this play is set over three hundred years ago. And it's based on real events. Can anyone tell us what happened back then?"

I actually knew all about what Ms. Gonzalez was referring to, since I'd written an essay about it last year in American history, and it was fascinating. So I put up my hand.

Ms. Gonzalez didn't turn cartwheels, but she beamed at me. "Yes, Kiara?"

I could practically recite my essay from memory. "In colonial Massachusetts, the Salem witch trials took place between February 1692 and May 1693. Hundreds of people, mostly women, were accused of being witches. There were trials, and thirty people were found guilty. Nineteen of them were put to death by hanging. According to sociologists, this was a notorious case of mass hysteria."

I could have gone on and given the names of all the executed people, but Ms. Gonzalez put up her hand.

"This is all very interesting, Kiara, and I'm sure everyone would like to know more, but we don't have much time and we need to get back to the play itself."

Usually, I don't like being interrupted when I'm talking, but I couldn't say that to a teacher. Actually, I wasn't surprised that she cut me off, and it didn't hurt my feelings. Like I've said, I can go on and on about a subject that interests me.

"Let's talk about the characters," Ms. Gonzalez said. "Who do you think is the hero of the play?"

Everyone pretty much agreed that it was John Proctor, because at the end of the play he wouldn't accuse anyone else even though he knew he'd be hanged for witchcraft.

"Only he wasn't perfect," Emily Baron said. "He was kind of a bully, the way he treated his servant, Mary."

"But there were worse bullies," Jim Berger pointed out. "Like Reverend Parris. He bullied his daughter and Abigail, his niece."

Ms. Gonzalez nodded. "And what about that niece, Abigail? Doesn't she bully all the other girls, threatening them, lying, telling them what to do?"

I nodded in agreement along with most everyone else. I'd found Abigail to be seriously annoying.

Ms. Gonzalez continued. "About the plot. What kicks off the situation? Alyssa?"

Alyssa hadn't raised her hand. She rarely does. She's smart, but she acts like she's not interested in anything that goes on in class. I think it's part of her goth act. But she does respond when she's called on.

"Reverend Parris sees a bunch of girls out dancing in the woods, and he thinks maybe they're witches."

Ellie added to this. "Or possessed by witches, and practicing witchcraft."

"Exactly," Ms. Gonzalez said. "And this becomes the question that the community confronts. Is someone a witch, or is someone the victim of a witch?"

After talking about the plot, Ms. Gonzalez asked what we thought of the trial.

"It wasn't very fair," someone in the back called out.

I could certainly agree with that. There was no evidence of any crime, and the so-called witches didn't have any real defense. Clearly, a lot had changed between then and *Courthouse Chronicles*.

When the discussion was finished, Ms. Gonzalez glanced at the clock. "We still have a few minutes left. Let's talk about some of the interesting T-shirts you've worn today. Alex, your shirt is very funny. Would you please stand up and let the others see it?"

Alex's T-shirt showed an oven. In the oven window, a chicken was roasting. In front of the oven, three live chickens looked frightened. Under the picture were the words A CHICKEN HORROR MOVIE.

Everyone laughed, and I could join in this time, because it really was funny.

"And Jim, could you tell us about your T-shirt?"

Jim Berger stood up. "Some people say that hugging a tree is good for your health, that it can make you feel calm when you connect with nature. But it's also a metaphor."

Ms. Gonzalez looked pleased. We'd talked about metaphors in class. "Go on, Jim."

"It's like, you don't have to actually hug a tree, but you should feel warmly toward trees. You should appreciate the importance of the ecosystem and show that you care about the earth."

"Very good," Ms. Gonzalez said. "Now, before we begin our next module, I'm giving you the opportunity to read something for pure enjoyment. I'm handing out a reading list, and you can choose whatever you want from it."

The lists were passed around. I stuck mine in my backpack, and then the bell rang. As usual, Ellie and Rachel and Alyssa and I gathered to leave the room together.

Paige Nakamura passed by. She wore a T-shirt with the words QUEEN OF THE GALAXY in sequins. That seemed appropriate, since she's a snob and always acts like she's the queen of something. And she is actually considered the most popular girl in the seventh grade—something I can never understand. But she probably figured that made her the queen of the class.

Normally, she doesn't speak to us unless she has something nasty to say, and today she did.

"You ever go dancing in the woods with other witches, Alyssa?" she asked.

Her little group of snobby friends giggled.

Alyssa replied. "Not lately, Paige. Are you inviting me?"

There was no response to that, and the Paige clique disappeared in the crowd that filled the hall. Out there, I got my first good look at the T-shirts my friends were wearing. Ellie's red T-shirt had a peace symbol. Alyssa's was black with white lettering: ZOMBIES EAT BRAINS SO YOU'RE SAFE. Rachel's read LA JEFA. I figured that was Spanish.

"What does it mean?" I asked.

Rachel looked mildly unhappy. "'The boss.' Mami gave it to me so I had to wear it. I wish there weren't so many people here who speak Spanish. Somebody's sure to tease me about it."

"Maybe they'll think you're calling yourself the boss because you're the seventh-grade rep," Ellie suggested.

Rachel shuddered. "But I don't want anyone to think I'm going to start bossing them around."

Alyssa uttered a short laugh. "I don't think you have to worry about that. You're not exactly the bossy type."

Personally, I thought Alyssa's shirt was perfect for her, since she doesn't like a lot of people. And I thought Ellie and Rachel should exchange shirts, since Ellie *is* the bossy type and Rachel is very peaceful. But since I've been trying to be more conscious of how I speak, I didn't say this. They might think I was insulting them.

We had to separate to go to our next classes, but Ellie and I were heading in the same direction.

"I have to tell you something," she said. "I looked in the spyglass this morning and saw you!"

"Playing with animals?" I asked.

"No. You were standing alone, with people all around you."

"What kind of people?" I asked.

"Kids. Like us. They were pointing at you."

I shrugged. "Okay."

"They weren't laughing, or even smiling," Ellie

continued. "It was like they were angry at you. Or accusing you of something. What do you think it meant?"

"I don't know," I said, but I did. And I wasn't at all comfortable with this. A memory was tickling the back of my mind.

"Well, it must mean something," Ellie insisted. "Those visions always do."

Fortunately, by that point, we'd reached the end of the hall, where we'd be going in different directions.

"Not this one," I said. And I hurried away.

three

AFTER SCHOOL, IN THE TURRET ON THE TOP
floor of Ellie's house, we went through our usual
routine. We peeled off our jackets, dropped our
backpacks, and took turns looking through the spyglass. I went first, and I didn't see anything unusual.
The others didn't see anything interesting either.
This is how it works—sometimes there are visions,
sometimes it's just an ordinary telescope.

I was actually relieved that there was nothing to
see this time. After what Ellie had told me she saw

that morning, I'd been afraid that Rachel or Alyssa would see it too—me, surrounded by people pointing at me. Every now and then, I saw Ellie glancing at me with a curious expression. I knew she was thinking about what she'd seen and wondering what that vision meant.

Having seen nothing to discuss in the spyglass, we turned our attention to the snacks Ellie had brought up for us. Ellie's parents are great about providing goodies—a little excellent junk food like chips or pretzels, brownies or cookies, plus fruit, and sometimes guacamole or salsa with carrot or celery sticks to dip into it. And they had let Ellie fix up the turret like it was her own private space, with big beanbag chairs and posters on the wall.

"Doesn't it ever bother your parents that we're here all the time?" Alyssa asked Ellie.

Ellie shook her head. "They never use this room. And they're happy I've got friends. With both of them working and my sister away at college, they were afraid I'd be lonely when we moved here."

"And they trust you on your own," Rachel said with a little note of envy in her tone.

"Well, Dad's usually downstairs in his office if we need an adult for something."

"But they give you privacy," Rachel pointed out. "If we were meeting at my house, Mom or Mami would be checking in on us all the time."

"And we wouldn't want to hang out at my place," Alyssa said. "It's too noisy. My stepbrother always has friends hanging around, and those guys are *loud*. My stepsister plays her ice-skating music full blast."

"Your stepsister ice-skates in the house?" Rachel asked.

Alyssa shot Rachel one of her famous eye rolls. "*No.* She just likes to listen to the music and visualize doing her routine. And my little brother plays video games with lots of sounds."

"Can't he use a headset?" I asked. "That's what *I* do."

"No, my mother, the great Dr. Khatri, won't let him. She thinks it can damage his eardrums. Of course, all the noise has to stop when my mother and stepfather are home," Alyssa said. "But then we have to deal with *them*."

"They're not nice?" Rachel asked, looking a little concerned. None of us have ever met Alyssa's parents, so we only know what Alyssa tells us about them.

We got another eye roll from her. "They want to be *involved*. It's so annoying. They'll ask you a million questions about your lives, like they're really interested."

"Maybe they are," Rachel ventured, but I shuddered. I wouldn't want anyone asking me a million questions about my life.

"It doesn't matter," Ellie said. "We can't meet there anyway. The spyglass is *here*."

Rachel sighed. "It's too bad we don't have magical binoculars, something portable we could take to each other's homes."

Ellie grinned. "Why? You don't like meeting here?"

"Of course I like meeting here," Rachel declared. "But my mothers are still happiest when I'm home."

We'd finished the snacks by now, so it was time for another look through the spyglass. This time Alyssa went first. She moved the spyglass to survey the town, and then, suddenly, she let out a cry. We all jumped up.

"What?" we cried in unison.

"There's a fight going on in the playground!"

We gathered around and she stepped aside to let each of us take a look. Rachel went next.

"It's a bunch of guys beating up on another guy. They look like they could be our age." She adjusted the magnifying dial. "I can't make out their faces."

"Let me look?" Ellie asked. She squinted as she

peered through the eyepiece. "The boy that's getting beaten up, he's wearing a green T-shirt." She turned the telescope over to me.

My eyesight is even better than Ellie's. "The T-shirt has a picture of a tree on it. It looks like the T-shirt Jim Berger was wearing today."

"Is it Jim?" Alyssa asked.

"I can't tell for sure," I said. "The other boys are blocking the view. Okay, I can see him now. He's short and skinny, and he has brown hair. I think it really might be Jim."

Ellie headed to the door. "I'm going to go down and tell my father. He'll call the police."

"Wait!" I yelled. "It's fading." And after a second I added, "It's gone."

"It wasn't real?" Rachel asked.

I shook my head.

Relieved, we all sank back down on the bean-bags. Ellie passed around the apple juice, and we filled our cups and drank thirstily.

"Well," Alyssa said, "that's okay, then. I know kids can get into fistfights sometimes, but I've never seen a bunch gang up on one person."

Rachel looked thoughtful. "I wonder what it meant. Every time we've seen a vision, it turned out to mean something, you know? Like, how someone was feeling, something they might be worried about. Or something that's going to happen, or something that happened before."

"Not always," I said, maybe too fast. So I quickly added, "You think some boys want to beat up Jim Berger?"

"Or maybe Jim *thinks* people want to beat him up," Alyssa suggested.

"But why?" Ellie wondered out loud. "Jim's a nice guy. He's a pretty good friend of Mike's."

"Mike Twersky, your boyfriend?" I asked.

"C'mon, he's not my *boy*friend," Ellie retorted. "He's a friend."

"And a boy. And you like him. And he likes you. Which makes him what?"

Ellie did a pretty good imitation of Alyssa's eye roll. "Whatever."

Like Alyssa, I have a hard time understanding Ellie's relationship with Mike Twersky. He's one of *them,* the others. He's popular. At lunch in the cafeteria, he sits with a bunch of popular seventh-grade boys.

But he's also nice. He does bird-watching, which isn't exactly a favorite hobby with the popular crowd. And once, in the cafeteria, he stopped one of his so-called cool lunch friends from tripping a younger kid. Plus, he has friends who aren't part of the popular crowd, like Jim Berger. And Ellie.

I figure he's just an exception to the rule of middle school popularity.

"Anyway," Ellie said, "I can't imagine anyone being angry enough at Jim to want to beat him up."

Neither could the rest of us, so we were all puzzled by the vision.

"But we don't really *know* Jim," Ellie continued. "I suppose I could ask Mike about him. But then he'd want to know why I was asking."

"And you can never tell him about the spyglass," Alyssa said, with a warning look.

Ellie shook her head. "Of course not!"

We didn't have any more time to do another spyglass survey. Rachel's mom came to pick her up, and she offered Alyssa and me rides home. It had gotten a lot cooler outside since the morning and there were some dark clouds, so we accepted the offer.

My father wasn't home yet, but Ms. Cavendish was there, and she called out from the kitchen to greet me.

"Hello, Kiara! Wait till you see what I have for you! Don't come in here, I'm mopping."

She emerged with a plate in one hand and a cup in the other and placed both on the dining room table. Joining her, I saw that the cup contained hot chocolate with little marshmallows floating on top, and the plate held three oatmeal cookies with raisins, which are my favorite cookies.

But after all the snacks at Ellie's, I didn't want to eat anything. It was on the tip of my tongue to say, "I'm not hungry." This had happened before, when I came home from a Spyglass Sisterhood gathering and Ms. Cavendish had prepared something for me. I'd told her I wasn't hungry. Dad had been there, and he gave me a stern look. I added "No, thank you," but that wasn't enough, according to my father.

After Ms. Cavendish left, he told me I needed to act more appreciative of her, that I should try to eat a little or I could hurt her feelings. I didn't really understand why not eating would hurt her feelings, but my father knows more about this stuff than I do, so I accepted that.

So this time I said, "Thank you," dropped my backpack by a chair at the dining table, and sat down. She smiled, said, "You're welcome," and went back into the kitchen.

I'd have to eat at least one cookie so I'd leave some crumbs as evidence. But as soon as she was out of sight, I wrapped the other two in a napkin and put them in my backpack for later. While the backpack was open, I pulled out my books and the other stuff that had been in my locker.

There were a couple of things in there that I hadn't put in the locker. At school, sometimes the office sends student workers around to put notices and things in all the lockers. Today, there was *Eastside News,* the school newspaper, and what looked like a flyer.

The newspaper comes out every Tuesday. Normally, I don't bother to read it because there's never anything interesting in it. But just to have something else to do while I tried to eat the cookie and drink the chocolate, I laid it on the table next to the plate.

It was all the usual stuff. A report on a soccer game. An announcement for Drama Club auditions. An interview with a teacher who isn't one of mine, so I wasn't curious.

I turned to the small flyer. I doubted it would hold anything of interest either, but it was kind of odd. In all capital letters, it read LAKESIDE LOONIES! ITS ON NOOZ! CHECK IT OUT!

The notice wasn't on the usual paper with the East Lakeside Middle School heading. And the missing apostrophe in *its* told me it wasn't from the office.

Ms. Cavendish reappeared. In my perusal of

the newspaper and the flyer, I'd actually eaten one whole cookie and I'd drunk all the chocolate, and I could tell this must have pleased her because her smile was wider than usual. I started to gather the plate and cup.

"Leave it, dear, the floor's still wet," she said.

"Okay," I said. And then, "Thank you. I'll go do my homework now."

I grabbed the newspaper, the flyer, and my backpack and went to my room. The newspaper was delivered to the wastebasket, but I held on to the flyer.

I didn't actually have any homework. There was a substitute in my last-period class who'd directed us to spend the time reading, so I did all the homework then. And I wasn't in the mood for a game on my laptop. My eyes kept moving to that flyer.

Lakeside Loonies. Loonies like lunatics? What could that mean?

I'd never heard of Nooz, but I figured it must be a new social medium. Like I said, none of us, the sisterhood, did any social media at all. But it wasn't like we'd taken a vow or anything. I was thirteen, so I could join this one without lying about my age, check out Lakeside Loonies, and then delete the app.

Or, if it turned out to be actually interesting, I could tell the others about it and maybe we could rethink our position on social media.

I got out my smartphone, went into the app store, and saw that Nooz was free. Not only that, but you only had to be twelve to join. Registering was no big deal, I didn't have to use my real name—I called myself SwanK, my old *Amazing Maze* name. Then I searched *Lakeside Loonies* and clicked to follow it.

There were only two posts. One was a photo of a teacher that someone had Photoshopped to add devil's horns. The other was a photo of Jim Berger in the T-shirt he'd worn to school that day. And under it, someone who called himself—or herself—the Champ had composed a message: *Berger has to hug trees because he has no friends.* A few people had added responses—a laughing emoji, *lol,* and *hahaha.*

The Champ. I remembered Rachel's T-shirt. LA JEFA. Didn't that mean "the champ"? No, it was "the boss." Besides, Rachel wouldn't post something like this. She never makes fun of people.

Then I thought about the vision of Jim through the spyglass. I wondered if this could have something to do with that. And I didn't delete my Nooz account when I finished reading the posts. I had a feeling I needed to keep an eye on this.

four

I DIDN'T REALLY THINK THE OTHERS WOULD scold me for looking at Nooz. They weren't like that. And after what we saw in the spyglass, I was very sure they'd be interested in the post about Jim Berger.

So the next morning, I accepted my father's offer of a ride to school so I could get there a little earlier than usual, and I waited for the others outside at the entrance. As students arrived, I found myself looking at each one who passed me and wondering if that person could be the Champ. To be perfectly honest, none of them looked like champions to me.

Ellie was the first of the sisterhood to appear. I told her I had some news to report, but I wouldn't talk about it until Rachel and Alyssa got there because I didn't want to have to tell the same tale twice. Ellie was impatient, as usual, but fortunately the others showed up just a few minutes later.

"Kiara has something to tell us," Ellie announced. Now they were all looking at me, like they expected something. That made me uncomfortable, since I don't like being the center of attention. So I averted my eyes and spoke in a rush. First, I told them about the flyer. It turned out that they'd all found the same flyer in their lockers, and they'd all been curious too, but they hadn't followed up on it because of our resistance to social media.

Still looking over their heads, I confessed to going into Nooz.

"I found Lakeside Loonies, and there was a picture of Jim Berger wearing that 'hug a tree' T-shirt, with a caption that said he had to hug trees because he doesn't have any friends, and a bunch of other people posted laughing signs like they agreed with that."

I was speaking so fast that I was out of breath by the time I finished my story. Then I checked their faces for reaction.

To my relief, they were all so intrigued by my report that they didn't care if I'd broken one of our rules.

"Why would anyone say that about Jim?" Ellie wondered aloud, shaking her head. "He's got friends."

"That's very weird," Alyssa agreed. "But people can be really nasty on social media."

Just then, Ellie's friend Mike Twersky joined us.

"Hey, guys," he said.

I liked the way he included all of us in his greeting and didn't just say hello to Ellie exclusively. Once again, I marveled at the fact that even though he was one of the popular kids at school, he didn't act like most of them.

"Hi," we chorused back, and then Ellie told him what I'd found on Nooz. Mike looked puzzled.

"That's strange. I'm not on Nooz so I didn't see it."

"He's your friend, right?" Alyssa asked.

Mike nodded.

"Well, your friend has enemies," she declared darkly.

Mike frowned. "He's never said anything about that to me."

We were then joined by another boy. I'd seen him around school before, but he wasn't in any of my classes so I didn't know his name.

Mike greeted him. "Thayer, my man, where have you been? What happened to you?"

So now I knew his name. He was kind of a big guy, and he was using crutches. One of his feet was in a cast.

"Yo, buddy," Thayer replied. Unlike Mike, he didn't greet all of us, and his eyes were only on Mike. "It happened Sunday. We were visiting my aunt and uncle and their house caught on fire. I ran upstairs to get their baby. But by the time I got there the fire had spread to the stairs. So I grabbed the kid and jumped out the window....Third floor," he added.

"Is the baby okay?" Ellie asked.

Thayer glanced briefly in her direction and then turned his attention back to Mike. "The baby's fine. I saved him."

"Wow!" Mike exclaimed. "You're a hero!"

"Yeah," Thayer said. "But I broke my foot. Now I'm off the soccer team."

Mike grimaced. "Too bad. You were a great goalie."

"Wait a minute," Ellie said. "This fire happened Sunday? I didn't see anything about it in the newspaper."

Thayer looked at her again. This time his expression was skeptical. "You read *newspapers*?" He spoke as if this was something unheard of that no normal person would ever do.

"My mother's a reporter," Ellie replied.

"Well, it wasn't in the newspaper," Thayer said. "They're keeping it quiet. For insurance reasons. So don't say anything to your mother."

That didn't make any sense to me. If these people had insurance, wouldn't they want to file a report so they could get the damage to their house repaired? I didn't say anything, though. This guy was making me a little nervous.

But Alyssa wasn't intimidated. "But how can they keep it a secret? Didn't neighbors see the fire? Didn't the fire department come? Where did this happen, anyway?"

Thayer's eyes narrowed. "That's none of your business!"

Alyssa shrugged. "I'm just curious."

"Well, don't be. Why don't you just crawl back into the cave you came out of, stupid witch."

At least, I *thought* he said "witch." He was a mumbler, so it might have been something worse. In any case, Rachel gasped, Ellie stared at Thayer with fire in her eyes, and Mike tugged on his arm.

"C'mon, man, bell's about to ring." As he pulled

Thayer away, Mike glanced back at us with an apologetic look.

"Are you okay?" Rachel asked Alyssa.

Alyssa gave a nonchalant shrug. "I've been called names before."

Rachel then turned to Ellie. "Thayer is so obnoxious! Why is Mike friends with a boy like that?"

Ellie sighed. "They've been pals since kindergarten, and their families are close. He knows Thayer can be rude, but Mike's loyal to friends."

We had to split up then to go to our respective homerooms, so we couldn't continue the discussion. The bell was ringing when I walked into my room, so I couldn't say anything to Jim. I wasn't sure if I should, anyway. If he knew what was on Nooz, he could be embarrassed. And if he didn't know, I didn't want to be the one to break it to him. I glanced over in his direction and saw that he didn't look any different from the day before, not upset or anything like that.

Later that day, in last period, the teacher was still absent and we had another substitute. Like the one yesterday, this one just told us to read and didn't pay any attention to what we were really doing. So I got out my phone, held it under the desk, and logged in to my Nooz account to see if there was anything more about Jim in Lakeside Loonies.

There was. It was a short video this time, and it looked like it was recorded during a boys' phys ed class. They were on the soccer field, and Jim appeared to have taken Thayer's place as the goalie. A ball came in his direction, he went for it but he missed it, and the ball went into the net. Under the video was the caption: *Worst Goalie Ever! Kick him off the team!* Once again, it was signed by the Champ.

What was really awful were the responses this time. Angry-face emojis, thumbs-downs, and comments: *What a jerk* and *Lose the loser* and *He screwed up.* The worst was an emoji I'd never seen before—a bunch of stick figures pointing at him with angry faces.

And then, suddenly, terrible memories of two years earlier came flooding back to me.

five

WE WERE LIVING IN THE TOWN I WAS BORN IN, which was pretty far from Lakeside. We had a nice little house with a garden. My father was a professor there too, at a different college. And Aunt Molly lived with us. She worked at a hair salon, but only in the mornings, so there was always someone there when I came home from school. Life was fine at home. But at Manchester Elementary School, life wasn't so good. Actually, my life there hadn't been good since kindergarten, but it seemed to get worse each year.

In the first few years of elementary school, I'd be invited to birthday parties, the kind where everyone in our class was invited. I didn't enjoy them very much. Being around a lot of people, with all the noise and running around, just didn't appeal to me. The games seemed so silly. I liked the cake and ice cream part, but that was all. Mostly, I spent my time at the parties hiding somewhere, or just sitting by myself. A parent would try to get me to join in with the others, but I just told them I preferred to be alone.

Before a party, Aunt Molly would take me out to buy a birthday present. She'd ask me what I thought the kid would like, but I had no idea since I never knew any of them very well.

"Then think about what *you* would like," my aunt suggested, but even back when I was five or six years old, I had a pretty strong feeling they wouldn't like the kinds of things *I* liked. Some of my favorite gifts were a kit of bones that you put together to form a complete skeleton, and a puzzle of a thousand pieces that took me months to complete. Or books.

I started reading before most kids. As soon as I learned the alphabet, I started looking at the daily newspaper and tried to sound out the words. I got magazines with word games and crossword puzzles. This was what I called fun.

I knew I was different. And everyone else did too. By fourth grade, kids were calling me names when teachers weren't listening: *weirdo, freakazoid, nutcase.* And *dummy,* which was really strange because I was very smart. I made all As. I got a prize at the science fair, and I won all the class spelling bees. But if we were playing a team game at recess, I was always the last to be picked. I didn't care because I didn't want to play anyway. And I always ate alone at lunchtime. If I tried to sit with people, they'd say "Go away," "Get lost," "Beat it."

Teachers usually liked me, though. I always did my work well, and if I was called on in class, I almost always got the answer right. If another student was called on and gave the wrong answer, I'd announce the right one. A teacher told me I should raise my hand first, but that seemed like a waste of time. Why should we have to wait to hear the right answer? But this gave my classmates another name to call me—*show-off.*

My fifth-grade teacher, Mr. Rush, gave me a lot of compliments on my work, and he said I had an excellent vocabulary. I wondered if maybe the other kids were jealous and that was why they were so mean to me.

One girl, Ashley, cornered me after class with a really ugly face and said, "You just think you're all that."

"All what?" I asked.

But she wouldn't tell me.

There was this one time when Mr. Rush was talking about Greek mythology. I had just read a book about this, a whole collection of stories. He told us about Pandora's box. Zeus, the king of the gods, had given her this box and told her never to open it. But she did, and all sorts of bad stuff came out—diseases, war, poverty. Mr. Rush said that this was how the people of that time explained why there was so much that was terrible in the world.

I raised my hand, and Mr. Rush called on me.

"There are lots of myths that explain why things happen," I said. "Like the myth of Persephone. It explains the seasons. Persephone was the daughter of Zeus and Demeter, who was in charge of agriculture. She was kidnapped by Hades, the king of the underworld. Her mother was really sad, and too depressed to let stuff grow. There was no harvest and people were hungry. So Zeus said she could have her daughter back. But there was this rule, if you ate something in the underworld you had to stay there forever...."

It was a pretty long story. *I* thought it was very interesting, but I guess some people were bored, and one boy started making noises like he was snoring. A couple of other kids were giggling, which didn't make sense to me because it was definitely not a funny story. Mr. Rush glared at them and shook his head, but then he interrupted me.

"It's a good story, Kiara, and I thank you for sharing it, but we really don't have time for more right now. Maybe you could tell the rest of the story to your friends at lunchtime."

But I couldn't, of course, because I had no friends and I was always sitting by myself at lunchtime.

Another time, when we were about to take a math test, Madison told Mr. Rush she didn't have a pencil. He asked if anyone in the class could lend her one. I always carried plenty of pencils, so I got one out and handed it to her. She took it, and then she went into her bag and brought out a packet of wet tissues for washing hands. She pulled one out and, while staring at me, began scrubbing the pencil furiously. As if I had germs!

Nothing made sense to me. I didn't *look* weird. I

wore jeans and T-shirts in warm weather, jeans and sweaters in cold weather, like everyone else. My hair was always nice and neat. But the girl who sat next to me, Chloe, was always trying to push her chair farther away from me. I was clean, I didn't smell, so once, I asked her why she did that. Did she hate me?

"I don't hate you," she said. "I just think you're creepy. Everyone does."

Aunt Molly would wonder why I never brought any friends home. I'd tell her I didn't have any friends. Then she'd get sad and want to talk to me about it, but I told her I wasn't sad at all, that I preferred to be alone. I never told her about how mean the other kids were, how they called me names, because that would make her even sadder.

It didn't bother my father that I wasn't bringing friends home. "You're a loner, like me," Dad said.

Since my father was a very smart and important person, I was pleased to hear that.

I was looking forward to middle school. I liked the idea of different teachers for each subject, and there would be a lot more students who wouldn't know about the names my elementary school class-mates had called me. But middle school turned out to be even worse.

In middle school, we didn't have recess, we had

phys ed. Every day, we had to change into these short blue uniforms in the girls' locker room and then play volleyball. There was no way to hide. Chloe from elementary school was in my class. On the first day, she didn't notice me. But on the second day, she saw me as I was undressing.

"You're wearing an undershirt!" she cried out.

Other girls turned to look at me, and I realized for the first time that they were all wearing bras.

Having not developed at all yet, I didn't see why my undershirt would be so shocking. "I don't need a bra," I replied, and didn't mention the fact that most of the other girls who were wearing bras didn't need them either.

"No boobs, huh?" Chloe said. I could see that she did have them, but I couldn't understand why that was something to be particularly proud of.

Another girl, whose name I didn't know, frowned at me and shook her head. "You'll never get a boyfriend if you don't have any boobs."

The other girls shrieked with laughter. So now I had a new name that people could call me. I'd be walking down the hall, and someone walking behind me would hiss "No Boobs" in my ear.

There was worse to come. On the very first day

in homeroom, the teacher handed out forms that we were supposed to read and sign and turn back in. The top of the paper read *Manchester Middle School Honor Code*. Basically, the code said that as students here, we promised we would not lie, cheat, or steal, and that we would not tolerate these behaviors in others. It added that we should report to a teacher any observation of these behaviors. Of course, I signed it, and looking around the room I saw that everyone signed theirs, including Madison, who was sitting next to me.

Our American history teacher, Mr. Henley, warned us on the first day of his class that we absolutely must read our daily assignments in the textbook and that he would occasionally give us pop quizzes in class. One week later, we had our first one.

I'd done the reading and the quiz wasn't very hard. I finished quickly and then spent a few minutes reading my answers over. As I was doing this, I became aware of Madison, leaning over from her seat to look at my paper. Quickly, I placed my hands over it. She turned away.

After I finished reviewing my work, I looked at her. Now she was leaning forward and peering over the shoulder of the boy sitting in front of her. She would look, then write something on her quiz, then look again and write something again. It was obvious that she was copying his answers.

I'd never thought of myself as a tattletale. But I'd signed that honor code, which meant I was obliged to tell Mr. Henley about what I saw. I did, he listened, and he thanked me. I had no idea what he would do about it.

I found out the next day. Chloe confronted me in the phys ed locker room.

"Did you turn Madison in for cheating?" she demanded. Her voice was loud, so now practically all the girls stopped talking and looked at me.

I could have denied it, but that would be lying. Lying, cheating, stealing...I'd signed that paper swearing I wouldn't do any of those things.

"Yes," I said.

"She was suspended for three days!" Chloe declared.

"Okay," I said.

If possible, Chloe's voice went even higher. "That's all you have to say? *Okay*? Aren't you even sorry?"

I shook my head. "I was following the Honor Code."

"You're a snitch!" Chloe shrieked.

Now all the other girls were glaring at me too. I couldn't understand it. Everyone in the school had read and signed the Honor Code. Was I the only one who would abide by it?

So now, along with *No Boobs,* I was called *snitch.* That very same afternoon, in the cafeteria, I had to pass Chloe while carrying my lunch tray. She was walking from the opposite direction and even though there was plenty of room to pass, she banged right into me, hard. I had to grab a chair to keep from falling, but my tray went flying and so did the food on top of it. It seemed like everyone in the cafeteria was watching, pointing, and laughing at me.

I felt sick. I ran from the room, the laughter following me. I considered going to the infirmary and claiming to be actually ill. But then my father or my aunt would be called, and how could I possibly explain this to them? So I just hid in a restroom for a while, until the end of the period, and went on to my next class.

That wasn't the end of my persecution, though. For the rest of the day and all the next, kids were whispering "Snitch" at me and giving me dirty looks. And on the third day, Chloe tried to trip me.

I was walking downstairs to get to a class, and there were at least a dozen others on the stairs at the same time. Chloe was just in front of me, and I saw her stick out her foot so I'd trip over it. I stepped around her, and in doing so, I must have surprised her and she lost her balance. Everyone on the stairs froze as Chloe tumbled down the steps. When she hit the bottom, she screamed.

A teacher appeared. "What happened?" she asked, and reached down to help Chloe up. Chloe pointed.

"She pushed me! Kiara Douglas pushed me down the stairs!"

"I did not!" I protested.

But now other kids chimed in to accuse me. "Yes, she did!" "I saw her!" "Kiara pushed Chloe!" "She did it on purpose!" They were all pointing at me.

Another teacher appeared, and between the two of them, they helped a limping Chloe away. Trying to ignore the taunts of the students, I went on to my next class. But news traveled fast. I'd just taken my seat when someone came in with a note for the teacher, who then instructed me to go immediately to the office.

When I arrived, the receptionist sent me into the office of the principal, Mrs. Forbes. I'd never encountered Mrs. Forbes up close. I'd seen her in an assembly, and a few times in the hallways, and she was always smiling. From behind her desk, she wasn't smiling now.

"Sit down, Kiara."

I did.

"I understand you pushed Chloe Matthews down the stairs."

I shook my head.

"But people saw you," she declared.

This time I managed a verbal response. "It was an accident. I didn't push her, she stumbled."

"Then why would other students say you pushed her?"

Because they don't like me. That was what I was thinking, but I didn't say it. It sounded so babyish, even in my head.

"I don't know."

Mrs. Forbes called my father and sent me back out into the reception area to wait. I had my back-pack with me, so I dug out one of my word game magazines and a pen.

"What are you doing?" the receptionist demanded.

"A crossword puzzle," I replied.

"This is no place for games!" she snapped. "Put it away."

So I was just supposed to sit there and stare into space? Fortunately, I didn't have to wait long. My father showed up, and I could tell he was upset. When he saw me, he asked, "What's going on?"

Before I could respond, the receptionist told him to go into Mrs. Forbes's office, and he did. He was in there for about ten minutes and returned with a different expression—angry.

"We're going home," he said.

We didn't speak in the car, but that wasn't unusual. My father liked to concentrate when he was driving. He must have called Aunt Molly to alert her, because she was waiting for us anxiously.

The three of us sat down at the kitchen table. Dad spoke first.

"Your principal says you're suspended for three days."

That was pretty much what I expected, so I just nodded. But my father wasn't finished.

"You didn't push that girl down the stairs, did you?"

"No," I said. "She was trying to trip me, and when I moved out of her way, she lost her balance and fell."

"And you told your principal it was an accident?"

"Yes. She didn't believe me. Because a bunch of other kids said they saw me push her."

"But why was she trying to trip you in the first place?" Aunt Molly wanted to know.

I told them how I'd reported on Madison and how she got suspended, that Chloe was her friend, how everyone was calling me names and giving me dirty looks.

"Did you tell your principal this?" Dad asked.

I shook my head. "It would only make things worse for me at school."

Aunt Molly stared at me. "What do you mean? Were they picking on you before all this happened?"

Finally, I told them what I'd been holding back from them for years, how kids had been calling me names in elementary school, how it was just as bad if not worse now in middle school.

"But why do they do this?" Aunt Molly asked.

I shrugged. "They don't like me. I turned someone in who was cheating. And I'm different."

They couldn't argue with that, but Aunt Molly was indignant.

"There's nothing wrong with being different! You're one of a kind, you're unique. That's a great thing!"

Dad nodded. "You've always had an unusual personality. Unusual in a good way," he added quickly. "Not like everyone else. Not ordinary."

"Not normal," I said.

He frowned. "Who's to say what's normal? You know, Kiara, there are students in my classes who play games on their mobile phones while I'm lecturing. When I told the dean about it, he said that was normal. That doesn't make it right, does it?"

I considered that. If they allowed us to have our phones out in middle school, I was pretty sure that was what a lot of students there would be doing too. But *I* wouldn't.

Aunt Molly turned to my father. "You should go right back there and confront that principal. How dare she accuse Kiara on the basis of a bunch of snotty little eleven-year-olds?"

My father shook his head, and I wasn't surprised. He always said he didn't like confrontations.

"I've got a better idea," he said. And he told us about a job offer he'd been considering. "It's at Bascomb College in Lakeside, on the other side of the state. It's a good position, I'd have the same rank and the same salary, but the cost of living is higher there. That's the one thing that's been holding me back from considering the offer. We might not be able to have a house as nice as this one."

"I know about Lakeside!" Aunt Molly exclaimed. "I have an old friend from school who lives there now, and she likes it a lot." She cocked her head thoughtfully. "And she told me the one drawback is the lack of a decent hair salon."

So the very next day, Dad withdrew me from Manchester Middle School. Since the new job wouldn't begin until January, he hired a tutor for me.

We would be moving to Lakeside in December, and I'd go to middle school there. Aunt Molly would be moving too, but she wouldn't be living with us. She was going to open her very own hair salon and live in an apartment above it.

I worried that the students in the middle school would be just as mean as the ones in the elementary school. Dad said the best way to keep this from happening was to be quiet at school and only speak when I was called on by the teachers. He told me I should be nice and polite, but I shouldn't expect to make friends with the other kids. He suggested that I just avoid even trying to get to know them.

So that's what I did at East Lakeside Middle School, all through the second half of sixth grade and the first half of seventh. Then Ellie and Alyssa and Rachel came along.

✦

The Spyglass Sisterhood wasn't going to meet that afternoon—Ellie had a dentist appointment. So I went straight home after school.

Ms. Cavendish wouldn't be making dinner for us that night. Dad taught a late class on Wednesdays, and he didn't come home till eight o'clock. Sometimes Aunt Molly would come over after she closed her salon, and we'd order food to be delivered. Then Dad would come home and we'd all eat our dinner in front of the TV and watch *Courthouse Chronicles* at nine.

Ms. Cavendish knew we ate later than normal on Wednesdays, so she always prepared a particularly good after-school snack for me. Today, there were her special apple and raisin salad, crispy cheese sticks, and chocolate chip cookies. As usual, it was way too much food, so I wrapped the cookies in a napkin and put them in my backpack for later.

Then I went to my room to do homework. I was in the middle of pre-algebra problems when my phone made a dinging sound. There was a message from Ellie to the sisterhood.

When I got home from the dentist, I looked in the spyglass and I saw Jim getting pelted with rocks! NR

NR meant "not real," that it wasn't an actual sighting, it was a vision. I tapped in my news.

There's a video of Jim on Nooz. He missed stopping a goal in soccer practice.

Alyssa and Rachel responded with frowning faces and question marks. Ellie wrote again.

We have to meet tomorrow!

We all sent thumbs-up emojis, and I went back to my homework. I'd just finished when Aunt Molly arrived.

"Hello, my favorite niece!" she greeted me.

She always says that, which is kind of silly since I'm her only niece. We said goodbye to Ms. Cavendish, and Aunt Molly went to the kitchen to pour herself a little glass of red wine. I took some grape juice. Then we settled down in the living room and waited for Dad.

"How are your friends?" she asked.

I'd told her about Ellie and Rachel and Alyssa, and she'd been happy that I'd made friends at school. Happier than Dad, I think.

"They're fine," I said.

"I'd like to meet them. Why don't you bring them by the salon sometime?"

"They're not African American," I told her. Aunt Molly's salon specialized in Black hair.

"I don't mean as customers," she said. "Socially! I could take a break and we could go to that nice little tea shop across the street from the salon."

I frowned. "I don't know if they like tea."

Aunt Molly sighed. "Oh, Kiara, don't be so literal."

She'd said that to me before, and I had looked up the word *literal*. The dictionary said it means "true, factual, not exaggerated." So what was wrong with being literal? I love Aunt Molly, but sometimes I don't understand everything she says.

Dad came home, we ordered pizza, and it arrived just before our TV show, which was perfect timing.

That night's case wasn't my favorite kind. I prefer trials where there are really bad people who do something terrible, or really nice people who are falsely accused of doing something bad. This case was about a man who was supposed to be a famous artist, and his paintings were worth lots of money. He was suing a newspaper that reported that he didn't really create his paintings, that he paid other people to paint them and he just signed them. Some of the newspaper readers believed this, and now he was selling fewer paintings.

The newspaper's defense team couldn't find anyone who'd been hired by the artist to paint his pictures, so I decided they'd made up that story about him and they should have to pay for it. But then it turned out that the artist had developed a condition that made his hands shake. He really couldn't paint anymore, and he *had* hired people to paint pictures in his style. So he lost the suit and the newspaper won the case.

We talked about it after the show.

"He should never have brought that suit," my father said.

"But it wasn't nice for that newspaper to print the story," Aunt Molly argued. "If a painting is pretty, and if it looks just like his other paintings, who cares who really painted it?"

Dad disagreed. "Customers are entitled to know the name of the artist. The newspaper was telling the truth."

At this point, I was getting a little bored, so I said good night and went to my room. But before going to bed, I checked Nooz one more time. There was another posting from the Champ. It was Jim's class picture from last year's school yearbook. The caption read *What a loser! Who wants to join the I Hate Jim Berger Club?* This was followed by the usual emojis, laughing faces, and thumbs-ups.

Jim was being bullied, I realized. Just like I was

bullied back in elementary school. But he wasn't like me at all—he wasn't so different from other kids. So why was he being treated like this? I wondered if his parents would take him out of school, like my father took me.

Maybe that was all you could do when you were bullied. Run away.

six

THE NEXT MORNING, I GOT TO SCHOOL A LIT-
tle early again, but this time I didn't wait outside for
the sisterhood. I went directly to homeroom.

Jim Berger was already there. Instead of going
to my own seat, I headed over toward him and sat
down at the desk next to his.

"Hi," I said.

"Hi," he replied, eyeing me warily. I wasn't
surprised—I didn't think I'd ever spoken to him
directly before.

Aunt Molly always says eating together makes

conversations easier. I reached into my backpack and pulled out a bulging napkin.

"Want a cookie? They're really good."

"Okay," he said. "Thanks."

I waited until he'd taken a bite, chewed, and swallowed. Then I plunged in.

"I saw the pictures of you on Nooz."

He nodded.

"I think you're being bullied," I continued.

He nodded again. "I guess so."

"So what are you going to do about it?" I asked.

He took another bite, chewed, swallowed, and said, "I don't know."

"You should tell someone," I declared.

He almost smiled. "I don't think that's necessary. Everyone knows."

"No, I mean someone in authority. Like a teacher. Or your parents."

He shrugged. "What good would that do? I don't even know who's posting that stuff."

"The Champ," I said.

"Yeah, but who's that? They can't stop the posts if they don't know who to blame."

He was making a good point.

"I've gotten other stuff too," he told me. "Notes in my locker. Prank phone calls."

"What do they say?"

He shrugged again. "Same kind of stuff. 'You're a loser.' 'Everyone hates you.' 'Drop dead.'"

"'Drop dead,'" I repeated. "That sounds like a threat. You could go to the police and they could investigate."

He shook his head. "That's just an expression. It's not like he said 'I'm going to kill you.'"

I caught a pronoun there. "Do you think it's a boy who's doing this?"

"I'm not sure. The person spoke in a funny voice, sort of high and squeaky so I couldn't recognize it. I guess I just assumed it was a boy."

"Girls can be mean too, you know," I said. "Like Paige Nakamura."

"Yeah." He almost smiled. "I once asked her if she'd sign a petition I was circulating to start a chess club. She called me a complete nerd." He looked at me with interest. "What you said about girls being mean too . . . have you been bullied?"

"Not here," I told him. "At my elementary school."

"What did you do?"

"Me? Nothing. My father took me out of school and then we moved here. Maybe if you tell your parents, they'll get you out of here."

Jim frowned. "But I don't want to leave East Lakeside."

"Why not?"

"Because I *like* this school! I like my teachers. Well, most of them. I'm on the soccer team and I'm goalie now, which is very cool. And my father can drop me off early, on his way to work, so I can be alone in homeroom and finish the homework I didn't have time to do last night. Why should *I* have to leave? That would be punishing me, and I haven't done anything wrong."

Those were all good reasons, I had to agree.

"Besides," Jim continued, "I think it's the bully who should be punished. Not the victim."

Another good point, I thought. But like he'd said before, the bully couldn't be punished if no one knew who he was.

Students were coming in now, so I had to go back to my desk. In the back of my mind, I pondered Jim's plight all morning. And at lunch with my friends, I reported what Jim had told me about the notes in his locker and the nasty phone calls.

"I wish we could find out who's doing this and then we could report him," Rachel said.

"But don't forget," I said, "there are people who agree with this bully. I told you about all the thumbs-ups he gets on Nooz."

"Then they're liking the posts because they like

the bully," Alyssa declared. "He must be one of the popular kids." She turned to Ellie. "Have you asked Mike about this? Mike's popular, maybe he knows who's posting those messages."

We all looked in the direction of the table where Mike always sat at lunch with other boys who were considered cool.

"Jim's not there," I noted.

"Jim's never there," Ellie told me. "He has a different lunch period. And Mike doesn't do Nooz."

"I thought all the popular kids were into social media," Rachel said.

"Mike's an exception," Ellie said. "I'll talk to him later and see if he's heard anything about this."

We planned to meet outside after the last class and walk together to Ellie's house. When I got to the meeting place, Rachel and Alyssa were already there. In the crowd lingering around the exit, we spotted Ellie talking to Mike.

"Maybe she's asking him about the bully," Rachel said hopefully. When Mike left, we made our way over to Ellie. She was smiling, and I hoped this meant she'd learned something from him.

"Well? What did he say?" Alyssa asked.

Ellie looked at her vaguely.

"Huh?"

I was getting better and better at reading people's expressions, and I realized that the smile on her face was the lovesick dreamy look she always had after seeing Mike.

"What did he say about Jim?" Alyssa asked with clear impatience.

"Oh! I didn't ask him. He was telling me he thought he saw a red-winged blackbird through a window in one of his classes."

"Ellie!" we groaned in unison, and she seemed to wake up.

"I couldn't ask about the bully, there were too many people around us. But he's coming over this afternoon to look for that blackbird through the spyglass. We can talk to him about it then."

♦

When we arrived at Ellie's we went immediately up to the turret so we could look through the spyglass before Mike got there. One by one, we surveyed Lakeside, but it wasn't until the last of us, Alyssa, had her turn that anything out of the ordinary was spotted.

"Paige Nakamura," she announced. "Crying."

Rachel took a look. "We've seen that before, haven't we? Like, ages ago?"

Alyssa nodded. "Yeah, and I still have no idea

why the Queen of Mean would have anything to cry about."

I took out my phone. "I'm going to check Nooz and see if there's another post."

There was. There was no picture this time, just text. *Let's take a vote! Who thinks Jim Berger is the biggest nerd at East Lakeside?* As usual, it was from the Champ.

"Take a look," I told the others, and they gathered around so they could see the screen. And reading it again, I gasped so loudly that everyone turned to me.

"What?" they asked in unison.

"I think, maybe, I know who the bully is."

"Who?" In unison, they all demanded to know the name.

"*Maybe*. I'm not absolutely sure...."

"Who?" they shrieked again.

I told them what Jim had told me in homeroom. "Paige calls Jim a nerd."

Rachel's eyes went wide. "Maybe that's why we've seen her crying in the spyglass! She's bullying Jim and she feels bad about it."

Alyssa shook her head. "Paige? Feeling bad about being nasty? I don't think so. Besides, would Paige call herself the Champ? I'm guessing she'd use 'the Queen,' or something like that."

But now Rachel was looking even more excited. "I'm just remembering something. It was after they made the rule about no words on T-shirts. Paige showed up in homeroom wearing a T-shirt with words in sequins."

"The one she wore on Tuesday?" Ellie asked.

Rachel shook her head. "No, a different one. It said 'The Champion.'"

Everyone fell silent as we considered this.

"I remember because it was a big deal," Rachel continued. "The teacher sent her to the office. And she had to go around the rest of the day wearing the T-shirt inside out so the words didn't show."

"I remember that too!" Alyssa exclaimed. "She started a whole fashion fad. All of a sudden girls started wearing T-shirts inside out."

"So she really could be the Champ," Ellie murmured.

But before we could talk about it, we heard the doorbell ringing downstairs.

"That must be Mike," Ellie said.

We followed her downstairs and to the front door.

Mike was his usual friendly self. "Hey, everyone. Want to look for birds with me? There's a blackbird I'm trying to spot."

"Let's have a snack first," Ellie said. "We want to talk to you about something."

"I already had something to eat at home," Mike said, but Ellie ignored that and led us into the dining room, where we all sat down at the table. There was a bowl of fruit there, and Ellie pushed it at me. I took some grapes and passed the bowl to Rachel.

Mike looked at us with interest. "You want to know something about birds?"

"No," Ellie said. "Well, not right now. We want to ask you about Jim Berger."

"What about him?"

"Remember I told you how someone posted something mean about him on Nooz? Well, it's getting worse. There are more posts and they're getting really nasty. He's getting notes and phone calls too. He's being bullied."

Mike's forehead puckered. I thought that meant he was puzzled.

"He hasn't said anything to me about it."

Alyssa turned to him. "You must have friends who are on Nooz. Haven't you heard anyone talk about the posts?"

Mike shook his head. "No. But people know I'm friends with Jim. Maybe they wouldn't talk about this in front of me. Who's writing these posts?"

Now the girls all looked at me.

"We're thinking maybe it's Paige Nakamura."

Mike didn't look shocked, but he still had those wrinkles on his forehead. "Yeah? Why do you think it's Paige?"

I quickly summarized the reasons—the fact that she called Jim a nerd, the words on the T-shirt that had to be turned inside out. Even as I spoke, I realized that this wasn't much in the way of evidence.

Mike shrugged. "Well, I guess it could be her. I mean, everyone calls her the Queen of Mean, right?" He grinned.

"It's not a joke," Ellie said sharply.

He held up his hands as if surrendering. "Okay, okay, sorry!"

Rachel leaned toward him. "You're friends with her, aren't you? Maybe you could talk to her, find out if she's doing this, and ask her to stop."

Mike's grin had completely disappeared. "I'm not going to start accusing someone of anything."

Alyssa was staring at him through narrowed eyes. "Do you really like those people?"

"Which people?"

"People like Paige. Or that creepy Thayer. Those snotty jerks you hang out with."

Mike stared right back at her. "You don't even know them."

"No, and I don't want to," Alyssa snapped.

Rachel's eyes darted back and forth between them. "C'mon, you guys, let's not fight about this."

Mike pointed at Alyssa. "She started it!"

Ellie let out a short laugh. "Mike, you sound like a little kid."

Mike didn't laugh. He turned to Ellie. "Do you agree with her?"

Ellie hesitated. "Well, sometimes I do wonder why you hang out with that crowd. I mean, *you're* not a snob."

"Are you saying *they're* all snobs? C'mon, Ellie. You're talking about my friends!"

"Then find out which one of them is bullying Jim," Ellie said.

"I'm not planning to run around giving my friends grief," Mike said sharply.

Alyssa spoke up. "It seems to me, Paige could use a little grief. She sure knows how to give it to other people."

Mike stood up. "Look, um, I gotta go."

"What about your blackbird?" Ellie asked.

"I don't really feel like looking for birds now." He started toward the door. Ellie rose and followed him. Back at the table, we heard her say, "So you won't do anything about this? You'll just let Paige ruin Jim's life?"

We heard the door open and shut. Then Ellie returned to the table. Her lips were trembling as she picked up a napkin. She turned away from us, but I could see her wipe her eyes.

I didn't know if she was crying for Jim or for Mike.

seven

I BROKE MY MORNING ROUTINE THE NEXT DAY. The very first thing I did, before I even got out of bed, was to grab my phone and check Nooz. I was hoping that maybe Mike had thought about what we told him at Ellie's yesterday. Maybe he'd reconsidered and talked to Paige.

But no. Not only were the posts still there, there was a new one from the Champ. It wasn't a photo of Jim this time. It was a shot of two men, standing by a car. One of them wore a police uniform. The caption read *Jim Berger's father gets arrested!*

There were a lot of emojis, too. Mostly faces with big *O*s for mouths.

There were other posts on Lakeside Loonies today. One was a photo of a hand with long red nails, and the caption read *Manicure*. Another was a guy I didn't recognize standing by a motorcycle with *My brother's new ride* under the photo.

The third one I saw had been posted by someone who called herself Sweetiepie. It was a photo of Paige and a girl I'd seen at school. Both were carrying a lot of bags and smiling happily. The caption read *Me and Paige, a haul at the mall.*

So this was what Nooz was for, I thought. Showing off, telling the world stuff no one else particularly wanted or needed to know. Now I really understood why the Spyglass Sisterhood avoided it.

I jumped out of bed, hit the bathroom, dressed rapidly, and got to the breakfast table even before my father was there. When he arrived a moment later, I was gobbling my cereal.

"Why are you eating so fast?" he asked.

I downed my orange juice in two big gulps. "I want to get to school early."

"I can drop you off."

"No thanks, I have to be there even earlier."

"Why?"

"There's someone I need to talk to."

He frowned. "Who? The principal? Kiara, are you having problems at school?"

I knew he wasn't referring to grades or schoolwork.

"No, someone else is. And I have to help him."

He was still frowning, not in an angry way. "Honey, be careful. You know that you have difficulty figuring out what people are feeling and thinking."

"I can tell that you're worried," I pointed out.

"I just don't want you jumping into situations where you may not understand what's going on, that's all."

"Dad, I know what I'm doing." Mentally, I added, *I think.*

He was still worried, I could see that, but I couldn't waste time convincing him that there was nothing to worry about. I grabbed my jacket and my backpack. I considered kissing him goodbye to reassure him, but since I don't usually do that, it would probably have the opposite effect.

I took off and walked very fast. When I arrived at school, the parking lot was filled with teachers' cars, but no one was dropping anyone off yet and there were no students congregating outside the entrance. The hall I walked down was silent.

As I'd expected, Jim was alone in our homeroom.

But this time he wasn't bent over a textbook. He was staring into space, and he must have been lost in his thoughts because he didn't even look up when I walked toward him.

Sitting down at the desk next to his, I didn't bother with any of the conversation openers that Dad had practiced with me over and over—*Hello, how are you, what's new,* all that stuff. I came directly to the point.

"I saw the new post on Nooz."

He continued to look away, at nothing, but he spoke. "And now you're going to ask me what my father did to get himself arrested. What crime he committed. If he's in jail now."

"No, that's not what I was going to ask you," I said.

He finally turned toward me so that I could see his expression, and I thought I identified something. The way his lips were pressed together tightly, the way he wasn't looking at me directly, but just to the side. I knew that look, I'd seen it on my own face in a mirror. He was trying not to cry.

"It's not true, you know," he said. "My father wasn't arrested. The cop in the picture? That's Marty Jackson. He's an old friend of my dad's, they went to school together. They saw each other in the parking lot at the mall and they stopped to chat. That's all."

"At the mall," I repeated. "So the bully must have been there too and took a picture."

"I guess. Did you see those responses to the post? Shocked faces. Now everyone thinks my father's a criminal."

"You have to tell everyone the truth," I declared. "Tell them who's bullying you."

"Yeah? How?" He looked away again and put a hand to his head like he had a headache. "Go around and ask people if they were hanging around in the mall parking lot around five o'clock yesterday?"

"You don't have to do that. I know who the bully is."

He turned back to me. "Who?"

We weren't supposed to use our phones at school, but the bell hadn't rung so it wasn't really school yet. I took mine out, went into Nooz, and found Sweetiepie's post again.

"Paige Nakamura was at the mall yesterday." I pointed to the time stamp. It had been posted the day before, at 5:15 p.m.

"Kiara, lots of kids go to the mall after school."

"They do?" I remembered the last time I went

to the mall, which was on the highway just outside town. It was last August, and Aunt Molly had taken me there to get some new sneakers. "Why?"

"To shop, I guess. Or just hang out in the food court. There's not much else to do in Lakeside after school. Unless you have a hobby or something. I play chess with a neighbor."

The mention of chess reminded me of the earlier post. "There was a post calling you a nerd. You told me Paige called you that when you wanted to start a chess club."

He shrugged. "I'm pretty sure there are other kids who think I'm a nerd."

I remembered Rachel's evidence and told him about Paige's "Champion" T-shirt. Again, he just shrugged.

"Paige isn't the only person who thinks she's a champion around here."

I nodded. He was right. That popular crowd, they probably all thought they were on top.

◆

At lunch that afternoon, I told my friends about the new post and how Jim wasn't convinced that Paige was the bully.

"We need more evidence," I told them. "What can we do?"

"Maybe the spyglass will show us something," Rachel said. She turned to Ellie.

"Are we going to have a spyglass session today?"

Ellie blinked. "Huh?"

Rachel repeated the question.

"I'm really not in the mood today," Ellie said. It dawned on me that she hadn't said much at all during lunch, which wasn't like her. Alyssa caught my eye and mouthed *Mike*.

"I can't come anyway," I told them. "I have an appointment with my aunt to work on my hair."

Rachel looked at me with interest. "What is she going to do to it?"

I shrugged. "Just the regular stuff she does every month. Conditioning, mostly. She calls it upkeep."

Now they were all looking at me with interest. "What would your hair look like if it wasn't braided?" Alyssa asked. "Like Dina Harris's?"

Dina wore her hair in a soft Afro that looked like a halo.

"Sort of. But not as nice." I decided to make a confession. "You know how some people bite their nails when they're nervous?"

Rachel immediately hid her hands under a napkin.

I continued. "Well, when I was nervous, I twisted my hair and got it all tangled and broken off. That's why Aunt Molly decided I should have braids. When I first got them, I picked them apart, but she yelled at me and told me she'd shave my head if I kept doing that."

Ellie's eyes widened. "Would she really do that?"

I shook my head. "She just likes to talk tough. Now I don't touch my braids. Mainly because it takes hours and hours to do them."

✦

Before I left school that afternoon, I stopped at the media center. Sometimes, Aunt Molly made me leave the conditioner on my head for an hour while she handled another customer. I needed something to read.

At the librarian's desk, I fished out Ms. Gonzalez's reading list from my backpack and handed it to Mr. Beckham.

"I need a book from this list. Like a biography."

Mr. Beckham scanned the titles. "These are all novels, Kiara. Fiction."

I made a face. "Anything with science in it?"

He perused the list again. "Wait here," he told me.

When he returned, he had a book in his hand. "Try this."

I read the cover out loud. "'*A Wrinkle in Time* by Madeleine L'Engle.' What's it about?"

"It's about some young people who go on a journey through space and time to save their father. There's science in it too."

It didn't sound too bad. I knew there was a movie, but I hadn't seen it.

"Okay," I said, and I remembered to add "Thank you." Which might have made up for the fact that I hadn't said "Please" when I first asked him to help me.

✦

Aunt Molly's hair salon was on Main Street. It was a pretty place, with light brown walls decorated with pictures of hairstyles in frames. They weren't from magazines—they were photos of styles that Aunt Molly had created. Customers could point at one of them and say "I want that."

There were lots of mirrors and shiny pink chairs positioned in front of sinks. Aunt Molly called them stations. When I arrived, my aunt was just spraying a lady's hair. It was pretty amazing, like a crown of curls and braids with beads woven in.

"Molly, you're an artist!" the woman exclaimed as she admired herself in a mirror. "A genius! This is worth every penny!"

"Glad to hear that," Aunt Molly said. "Because it's costing you a lot of them."

My father would have said this was a rude thing to say, but the woman laughed. Aunt Molly does charge a lot of money for her work, but her customers are always happy. I get styled for free.

Aunt Molly introduced me to the lady. "Angela, this is my favorite niece, Kiara. Kiara, this is Ms. Collins." As she spoke, she shot me a look. She knows I don't like meeting people, but she'd trained me how to do it.

"How do you do, Ms. Collins. Pleased to meet you."

Aunt Molly gave me a quick nod of approval. While she escorted Ms. Collins to the receptionist's desk, an assistant helped me into a white robe and showed me to a station. I dumped my backpack by the side of the chair and sat down.

Aunt Molly returned, pushing a cart full of hair products and positioning it by the station.

"How are you, honey?" she asked as she began examining my head.

"Fine," I replied, and remembered to respond with "How are *you*?"

"Just dandy," she said. "Your braids look good, I can see that you're not picking on them anymore." She applied some shampoo to the palms of her hands and began smoothing it onto my head. Aunt Molly likes to act tough, but she's actually very gentle, and her rubbing felt like a massage. I could feel myself relaxing, and I almost stopped thinking about Jim Berger and Paige Nakamura.

But then she asked, "How's school?" and it all came back.

"There's a bully," I told her.

Her hands froze. "Who's bothering you?" she demanded.

"Not me. Someone's bullying a boy in my class."

Aunt Molly resumed her massage, even more gently now. "This must bring back some bad memories."

"Yeah." I sighed. "I don't get it. Why do people act like that? What makes them want to bully other people?"

"I don't know," Aunt Molly said. "Different reasons, I think. Some people just don't like anyone who's different."

I couldn't accept that, not in this case. "But this guy at school, Jim, he's not different. He's just a regular person."

I could see Aunt Molly's face in the mirror, and she looked thoughtful.

"Well, I suppose there are people who just want

to feel powerful. Personally, I think maybe these bullies don't feel very good about themselves, so they look for someone they can feel superior to."

That didn't make any sense to me either. "But this bully, at least the person I think is the bully, she's the most popular girl in the seventh grade. Kids at school think she's cool. She likes herself a lot."

"Well, maybe she's just plain mean. Some people are, you know."

She was right about that. And some of the other popular kids, like Paige Nakamura, are pretty mean. Like that friend of Mike's, Thayer.

"So how can you stop a bully?" I wondered. I didn't even realize I'd spoken out loud until she replied.

"I don't know. I guess the best thing is to just stay away from them."

"That's why Dad took me out of Manchester School, right?"

"Yes."

I considered that. Of course, if you could avoid bullies, they couldn't bully you. Only then they'd just find someone else to bully.

"But wouldn't it be better if you could stop them from bullying anyone?"

Aunt Molly didn't reply. She pushed my chair around and pulled a lever so the back of the chair tilted and my head rested in the sink.

"I'm rinsing now," she said.

I closed my eyes and enjoyed the warm water running over my hair. After a minute, she wrapped my head in a soft towel.

"I'll bet you've never been bullied, Aunt Molly."

"No."

"Was Dad?"

"Hush, I'm concentrating." She began applying the conditioner to my hair. This is my favorite part because the cream smells like roses. Once my hair was coated to her satisfaction, she spoke again.

"Once, when your father and I were in elementary school, there was a boy who picked on your father."

"What did the boy do to him?"

"Oh, silly stuff. He'd knock your father's books off his desk. Once, he hid your father's sneakers in the locker room so he couldn't go out and play games at recess. And he called him egghead."

"What does that mean?"

"It was a name kids called someone who was very smart and read a lot."

"But that's a compliment," I pointed out.

"Not the way that boy said it."

I got it. In pre-algebra, when I answered a problem correctly, there was a boy sitting behind me who muttered "Know-it-all." Now, if he was simply saying I understood everything about algebra, it would be a compliment. But I knew the boy didn't mean it that way.

"How did that make Dad feel?" I asked.

"Embarrassed." And then she added, "Sad. Your father didn't try to be popular. But he didn't want people making fun of him either."

So what did Dad do about it?"

"Nothing."

"Nothing?"

"Your father likes peace and quiet, Kiara. You know that. He doesn't like confrontations and he doesn't want to fight with people."

"So that's why Dad took me out of that school. Because he didn't want to fight with those people who didn't want me there."

I'd never seen Aunt Molly fight with anyone, but I'd certainly heard her have confrontations. I remembered once in a coffee shop, when a waiter brought her the wrong thing. I almost felt sorry for him.

"You're not like that," I said.

"No, I'm not. And I told that boy in elementary school to leave my little brother alone or he'd be very sorry. I was bigger than him and I scared him. He thought I was going to beat him up."

"Cool," I said.

"No, not cool. I was threatening him. I made it sound like I could get violent. And that's never the way to resolve problems. I'm rinsing out the conditioner now."

While I was under the warm water again, I considered what she'd said. And when I was once again wrapped in the towel, I said, "There are ways to fight without using violence. Dad's smart. Couldn't he have argued with those people at Manchester? Told them how they should believe me?"

Aunt Molly went quiet. She unwrapped me and began to apply the final treatment, a moisturizer. This smelled like lavender. Then she put a bonnet over my head and looked at the clock on the wall.

"Forty-five minutes," she said.

"Aunt Molly? Why didn't Dad argue with them?"

"Honey, sometimes you have to choose your battles and decide if they're worth the effort. You were very unhappy, and your father thought the most important thing was just to protect you."

"Did you agree with him?"

She smiled softly. "Your father and I are very different people, Kiara." As she wheeled over a hair dryer, I reached down and retrieved my book from my backpack. She placed me under the dryer and turned it on, and now there was no opportunity for more conversation.

I opened the book and began to read.

eight

THE LAKESIDE LOONIES NOOZ ACCOUNT WAS getting more popular—I saw a bunch of posts Saturday morning. They were all pretty silly things about people I didn't know, and signed with names that meant nothing to me.

Corey D. got sent to the office yesterday. Anyone know why?

Coach Hixon has a girlfriend! I saw them at the mall!

Jessica P. stole my lip gloss!

And there was another post from the Champ:

Seen in the locker room—Jim Berger had his under-pants on inside out!

And there was a photo. I had to really squint to make out the fact that there was a label that would normally be on the inside of whatever someone was wearing. Plus, Jim's back was to the camera, so I couldn't even see his face. I figured that was why the Champ felt it was necessary to describe who was in the picture. I supposed that even if the underpants were on correctly, Jim would be embarrassed by a picture of him undressed like that.

Seriously dumb stuff. But there was also something weird about it. How did Paige see Jim like this? What was she doing in the boys' locker room? Maybe some guy told her about it and just passed along the photo.

I met with the sisterhood at Ellie's that afternoon. I was the last to arrive, and I couldn't show them the Nooz stuff right away. Alyssa was complaining about her mother.

"She wanted us to have a mother-and-daughter day today. Get manicures and go shopping."

"What's wrong with that?" Ellie asked.

"She'd try to make me wear pink nail polish when she knows I only wear black. And shopping? She'd insist on buying me a dress with pink flowers!"

I glanced at Rachel, who was wearing a pink flower–print dress that day. She just smiled and shrugged.

Alyssa continued. "She's always trying to make me change my look! And I won't give in to her! So I told her I already had plans for today and walked out."

She was pretty angry, and the other girls spent a lot of time consoling her. As for me, I couldn't stop thinking about what Aunt Molly had told me about my father. Personally, I didn't think it was so terrible to have someone call you a name that implied you were really smart. But my father must have felt the guy was mocking him, and that could have been humiliating.

When Alyssa finished talking about her mother, and we went downstairs to raid the refrigerator, I was about to break in with my Nooz news but Ellie started moaning about Mike. Alyssa and Rachel began offering advice.

"You have to forgive him, Ellie," Rachel said as she poured a bag of popcorn into a bowl. "He's torn between two friends. This has to be hard on him."

Alyssa extracted a large soda bottle from the refrigerator. "You're better off without him. I think maybe he cares more about birds than you, anyway."

It was like they'd forgotten what was really important here.

"I've got an idea," I proclaimed.

"About Mike and Ellie?" Rachel asked.

"No, about Jim! Listen. First off, make up a birth date so you can join everything, Nooz, Instagram, all that stuff. Then we ask everyone who likes Jim to put negative responses to Paige's posts."

"Kiara, we still don't know for sure that Paige is the bully," Rachel reminded me.

"Yes, I know, you're right. So we ask everyone to put negative responses to the Champ's post, who-ever it might be."

But Rachel shook her head. "I'm not thirteen and I don't want to have to lie about my age," she said softly.

Alyssa too was shaking her head. "Forget it," she said flatly. "There's no way I'm going to get into social media."

"Okay," I said, "then we contact people another way. We talk to them at school, we put notes in their lockers."

Alyssa wasn't any more enthusiastic about that idea. "Like anyone's going to listen to us?"

Rachel agreed. "Whoever's writing those posts is probably someone from the popular crowd, Kiara.

Someone who's got lots of friends. We don't. We can't influence people the way the Champ does."

Even though I didn't particularly want to talk to kids at school, I was getting annoyed. They weren't even considering my plan. "You got any better ideas?"

We stood there, holding the snacks, and the others were looking at me oddly. My annoyance had to be showing in my expression.

"Let's go upstairs," Ellie said.

They started moving in that direction, but I remained still. What I really wanted to do was show them how angry I was by walking out of the house.

"Kiara?" Rachel asked. "Aren't you coming?"

I almost said no. But then I thought back to those lonely days before I was brought into the Spyglass Sisterhood. And I couldn't let one disagreement send me back there.

Still feeling disgruntled, I followed them to the turret. We spread out the snacks on the rug, and Ellie went to the spyglass.

"Anything there?" Alyssa asked.

"Paige Nakamura."

"That's the third time we've seen her," Rachel said.

"Wait, there's someone with her," Ellie said. "It's Thayer!"

"Then it's real life," Alyssa said. "They're probably friends."

"But she's crying again," Ellie reported. "And... oh, he's throwing rocks at her!"

We all gathered around to take a look. And we each saw Thayer throwing rocks at Paige.

The vision faded away.

"What did *that* mean?" Alyssa wondered out loud.

I pondered this and came up with an idea. "She's bullying Thayer, too. And he's mad at her."

"I'm confused," Rachel said. "Aren't they both in the same crowd? Why would she bully Thayer?"

"Who cares?" Alyssa replied. "He deserves to be bullied."

I glared at her. "No one deserves to be bullied!"

I must have spoken very loudly and with a lot of emotion, because everyone was now staring at me.

"Sorry," I murmured.

"Don't be sorry," Ellie said. "You were expressing how you feel." After a second, she added, "And I think maybe you've been bullied too. Am I right?"

I didn't answer.

"Why would Kiara be bullied?" Rachel asked.

"Because she's different," Ellie replied.

Rachel wasn't satisfied with that. "We're all different."

Alyssa nodded fervently. *"I've* been bullied. Not as bad as Jim. But kids have called me a witch, or a vampire. And Rachel, you've been called names too. I've heard kids call you teacher's pet."

"Other names too," Rachel told us. "Last year, Paige Nakamura noticed that Mom picked me up from school every day, and she made fun of me, loudly, so everyone could hear. She asked if Mom held my hand when we crossed streets."

"Ellie, were you ever bullied?" I asked.

"Yeah, at my old school. When my parents were campaigning to have a homeless shelter built in my hometown. Adults were angry at them, and their kids started picking on me. Even the kids I hung out with."

With all their confessions, I decided it was time to make mine.

"I was bullied. In elementary school, and when I started middle school back in Manchester." I told them about the classmates who called me names and how they accused me of pushing a girl down the stairs.

"It wasn't true," I told them. "But the principal didn't believe me and I was suspended. At least my father believed me. He took me out of that school permanently so I wouldn't have to suffer there."

"But you were the victim!" Alyssa exclaimed.

"They should have kicked out those kids who were bullying you."

I agreed. "Unfortunately, the principal didn't hear people calling me names. But she heard them all say I pushed the girl down the stairs."

"It's hard for me to think of Thayer as a victim," Ellie mused.

"We need to find out for sure if Paige is bullying him," Rachel declared. "Because if we decide to report her to the principal, it would be good if we had more victims to name."

"We could just ask her," Alyssa said.

Ellie shook her head. "She won't talk to us at school. It could hurt her cool-girl reputation."

"We could go to her home," I suggested. "Ellie, do you have the school directory?"

"We don't need it," Rachel said. "I know where she lives."

I remembered when we learned through the spyglass that the lost dog Rachel had found and now loved had once belonged to Paige. Rachel had taken Fifi to Paige's house, but Paige's mother told Rachel to keep the dog since Paige didn't take good care of her.

"I know where she lives too," Alyssa declared.

"How?" I asked.

"I've been there. We used to be friends."

Our jaws dropped.

"Not *best* friends. Kindergarten through fifth grade, we were in the same class. I went to all her birthday parties, she came to mine."

"What happened?" Ellie asked.

"Middle school. She became cool, I didn't."

It was too late to go there today, so we agreed to meet and visit Paige the next day.

✦

At dinner that evening, my father asked the usual question.

"How's school?"

Usually, I just said "Fine." But this time, I told him about Jim and how we suspected a certain girl was bullying him.

He frowned. "Has this girl been bothering you?"

"No."

"Well, stay out of it. You don't want to draw attention to yourself. She could start bullying *you*."

"She shouldn't be bullying anyone, Dad."

"True," he admitted, and went back to his lasagna.

"Dad..."

"Hmm?"

"Why did you take me out of elementary school?"

"You know why. People were cruel to you."

"But that made it seem like *I* was being punished."

He stopped eating. "What are you talking about? That wasn't a punishment. You had to be glad to get out of there!"

"Yeah, but . . . maybe it was the others who should have been suspended. The ones who called me names and accused me. After I left, they probably just identified someone else to pick on."

Dad became very quiet. Finally, he said, "I did what I thought was best for you, Kiara. Maybe I could have done more, defended you, told the principal she needed to conduct an investigation into the matter. I don't know. But I just didn't want you to go on suffering."

I couldn't read his mind, and he wasn't saying how he felt. But somehow, I knew that at this particular moment, my father was very sad. So I did something I'd never done before. I got up, went over to his chair, and gave him a quick kiss on his cheek.

Then I went back to my seat and continued eating.

nine

ON SUNDAY, WE MET AT RACHEL'S IN THE afternoon. It was easier for her that way. With all of us there, her parents wouldn't ask a million questions about where she was going and why, the way they would if she was going out alone.

The Nakamuras didn't live far from Rachel, and we were in front of Paige's house in ten minutes. We started toward the front door, but just then a car pulled into the driveway. Right beside us, a woman got out of the driver's seat. Paige was getting out on the other side, and she didn't see us right away.

The woman smiled at us. "Hello, Rachel, nice to see you again. Can I help you girls?"

"Hello, Ms. Nakamura," Alyssa said.

The woman looked at her with no expression, but then, suddenly, her eyebrows shot up.

"Alyssa Parker? Hello! I haven't seen you in a very long time. You've... changed. Paige, look who's here!"

Paige came around the car and stopped short when she saw us. "What are *you* doing here?" she demanded.

"We came to see you," Alyssa replied.

Mrs. Nakamura drew her coat closer. "Well, don't just stand there, girls, it's chilly out here! Come inside."

For some reason, I remembered how I'd felt when watching a horror movie at home alone one night. I was pretty sure the expression on Paige's face was just like mine at that time.

We followed Mrs. Nakamura and Paige into the house.

"Can I offer you girls anything? Something to drink, a snack?"

"No, thank you," we all said.

"Okay, if you change your minds, just let me

know. Paige, why don't you take your friends down-stairs to the den."

Friends? I was surprised Paige didn't immediately correct her mother. But she just looked at us without smiling and beckoned us to follow her. We did.

The den was a paneled basement, with light coming in from windows high on the walls. There were a sofa and comfortable armchairs, but Paige didn't invite us to sit down, or even take off our coats. So we all just stood there and looked at her, while I surveyed the room and took in a massive TV and a Ping-Pong table and framed photos of Paige everywhere.

"What do you want?" she demanded.

Her question was greeted with dead silence. And for once, I wasn't the only one who couldn't make eye contact. No one was looking directly at Paige. It occurred to me that she would make a very credible bully. She was...I searched my mental dictionary for the right word. *Intimidating.*

I'd expected Ellie to kick off the interrogation, since she always tried to take the lead. But when she didn't speak up, I stepped forward and got right to the point. Focusing on the pink headband that adorned Paige's hair so I wouldn't have to look at her intimidating face, I asked, "Are you bullying Jim Berger?"

I assumed she'd immediately deny it—in *Courthouse Chronicles,* criminals always deny the crimes when they're first accused. Instead, her brow furrowed, which I knew was a sign of confusion.

"Who?" she asked.

"Jim Berger," I repeated.

She still looked confused.

Ellie spoke. "He's in our English class. Short, skinny, brown hair?"

Paige's forehead cleared. "Oh! The nerd."

"He's not a nerd!" Alyssa exclaimed. "He's a nice guy!"

Paige shrugged. "What was the question again?"

Ellie took over. "Are you bullying him? Are you posting nasty comments on Nooz?"

"No," Paige said.

I was puzzled by her nonchalant response. On *Courthouse Chronicles,* the accused would get upset and yell "That wasn't me!" or "I wasn't even there!"

"You're on Nooz, aren't you?" I asked.

"Of course."

"Then you must have seen those posts about Jim," Alyssa pointed out.

Paige shook her head. "I only follow the posts

from my friends. And we wouldn't be interested in anything about Jim Gerber."

"Berger," Ellie corrected her.

"Whatever."

"Well, someone's interested," I said. "And we think it might be one of the kids in your crowd. Do you know anyone called the Champ?"

Something changed. Instead of her snapping back at us, Paige's mouth fell open but no words came out.

Just then, Paige's mother came down the stairs with a pitcher of what looked like orange juice in one hand and a stack of paper cups in the other, and placed them on a table.

Beaming, she said, "I thought you girls would be talking up a storm here and you'd need something to refresh your palates!"

While my friends murmured their thanks and gathered around the table, my eye was caught by one of the photos on the wall. Actually, it wasn't a photo, but a framed clipping from what looked like a newspaper. The heading read *Kennedy Elementary School Bowling Team,* and the eight kids in the picture looked around ten years old.

I thought I recognized Paige, and some of the others looked familiar. A boy in the center held a trophy. I looked at the names listed under the photo and saw that I was right about Paige. But it was another name that sent shock waves through me, the name that identified the boy with the trophy.

Thayer "the Champ" Tillman.

"Don't you want any juice, dear?" Ms. Nakamura asked.

I turned. "No, thank you."

She smiled, nodded, and left. Then I turned to Paige and forced myself to look directly at her.

"It's Thayer, isn't it?"

She didn't answer.

"And he's bullying you too."

ten

PAIGE'S HANDS TIGHTENED INTO FISTS, AND now she was breathing rapidly. Those visions through the spyglass—Paige crying, Thayer throwing rocks at her—they made sense now.

When Paige finally spoke, she was almost stuttering.

"Why...what...what gave you that idea?"

Of course, I couldn't tell her what we'd seen in the spyglass. I pointed to the picture of the bowling team on the wall. "Thayer 'the Champ' Tillson."

Ellie turned to me. "Okay, maybe Thayer's the

bully. But he hasn't written anything about Paige on Nooz, has he?"

"There's nothing about me on Nooz," Paige retorted.

Alyssa jumped in. "No, it wasn't Nooz, Ellie." To Paige, she said, "We—we heard a rumor. At school."

"*You* heard a rumor?" Paige repeated, but she made it sound like we were so out of the mainstream that there was no possible way we'd ever hear about anything at school. "Who told you this?"

Since there really wasn't anyone at school who talked to us, I came up with an answer. "We were in the stalls, in the restroom. And we heard some girls come in, and they were talking about you."

That was pretty dumb, because I'd made it sound like the four of us had to use the bathroom at the very same time. But Paige didn't question that, and I must have made it sound believable because she sank down on the sofa and buried her face in her hands. Even though her mouth was covered, we could hear her crying. I glanced nervously at the staircase and hoped Paige's mother couldn't hear her too.

Rachel immediately sat down next to Paige and tried to put an arm around her, but Paige shrugged it off roughly. Ellie spotted a box of tissues on an end table and handed it to Paige.

I couldn't tell if Paige was angry or frightened. Maybe both.

Eventually, the sobs turned into whimpers. Paige blew her nose, wiped her eyes, and spoke.

"It started two months ago. Thayer invited me to go to the movies with him."

"What movie?" I asked with interest, but Alyssa elbowed me and hissed, "That's not relevant!"

Paige went on. "I told him I couldn't, that I was already doing something on Sunday. He told me I should change my plans and I said no. I guess that really pissed him off. He thinks a lot of himself, you know."

I nodded. "He's egotistical."

Paige looked up. "Huh?"

"Never mind," I said. "What happened then?"

"First he started lying about me, to my friends. Like, he said *I'd* asked *him* out, and when he said no, I started crying! And he started posting things about me on Instagram. He wrote that I was desperate for a boyfriend, that boys should stay away from me and girls shouldn't trust me."

"That's harassment," I said. "I think a person can go to a detention center for harassment."

"I don't want to put him in *a detention center,*" Paige said. "He's in our crowd. I just wanted him to stop posting about me and leave me alone. But then, the next week at school, he told Maria Guzmán that I had a crush on her boyfriend and that I was going to ask *him* to go to the movies."

"Maria Guzman," Alyssa repeated. "Isn't she one of your best friends?"

"Used to be."

Rachel looked shocked. "You mean she believed him?"

Paige nodded. "Now she won't speak to me. And some of my other friends told me I was getting a bad reputation."

Personally, I thought she already had a bad reputation, as the Queen of Mean. But I realized she was referring to a bad reputation among her friends, the ones she wasn't mean to.

"He's horrible," Ellie said. "I wonder if he's bullying other people too? He's really being nasty to Jim."

Paige shrugged. "That's different."

"Why?" Ellie demanded.

"Well, Jim's really a nerd."

I silently groaned, and for a moment I wondered if maybe Paige deserved to be bullied. No, not really. Even a mean girl shouldn't have to suffer like that.

Suddenly, Paige stood up. "Look, if you tell anyone about this . . . a lot of my friends know, but I don't want the rest of the school to find out. They look up to me."

"We wouldn't tell anyone," Ellie assured her.

"And don't tell anyone you were here and I talked to you."

Alyssa gave Paige a look I've come to recognize—narrow eyes, tight lips. It was a look I would never want directed at me. And since there was no reason to stick around and Paige clearly didn't want us there, we left.

✦

"I don't know who's worse," Ellie said as we were walking down the street. "Thayer or Paige."

"Thayer," Rachel replied. "He's terrible. Like a criminal. Paige isn't nice, and I don't like her, but she's still a victim."

All the way back to Ellie's, we talking about what we could do with this new information. We now knew for sure that Thayer was the bully. But what could we do about it?

Up in the turret, Rachel went to the spyglass.

"See anything?" Alyssa asked.

"Yes. Some guys kicking a ball around."

"So, not a vision," Ellie said.

"Wait, I think it is. I've never seen this place before. It looks like a basketball court. But they're playing soccer on it."

That didn't sound very interesting to me. But Rachel's next remark did.

"Oh! One of the boys is Thayer!"

"He's playing soccer on crutches?" Ellie asked.

"No, he's not on crutches here. I think this is a vision!"

The rest of us gathered around, and Rachel handed the spyglass to Alyssa.

"I know that place," Alyssa remarked. "It's a playground on the other side of town. My stepbrother has a friend there, Greg Tillman. Yeah, I see Greg now!"

"Tillman," Ellie echoed. "That's Thayer's last name. Maybe that could be the cousin whose house burned down. Ooh, maybe we're going to see the fire and Thayer saving the baby!"

But that wasn't what we saw at all. Rapidly, we passed the spyglass back and forth. I was the lucky one who caught the big moment. Thayer was running toward the ball and two boys charged him. Thayer went flying through the air and hit a metal post.

"Ouch!" I cried inadvertently.

Alyssa snatched the spyglass from me. "Wow, I think he's really hurt! He's holding his foot."

Ellie got it next. "It looks like he's screaming! Now some adults are running onto the court. It's fading now."

Something occurred to me. "Do you think…"

Alyssa finished my thought. "That's how he broke his foot? And he made up that story about the fire and saving the baby?"

Rachel joined in. "And he doesn't want people to know he broke it playing soccer?"

"Because he thinks he's a star player," Ellie said. "I guess we're seeing what really happened."

Alyssa rolled her eyes. "It's so silly, that's nothing to lie about. I mean, even professional athletes get injured. It's not a big deal."

"We can make it a big deal," I declared. "You know what this is?"

"What?" Rachel asked.

I smiled. "Ammunition."

eleven

ON MONDAY MORNING, I SAW TWO NEW POSTS from the Champ. One of them was about Jim.

Know why Jim Berger gets good grades? He cheats! I've seen him!

The other post was about someone I didn't know.

Olivia Kelly is a fat ugly pig! I think we should all start chasing her home from school. She needs the exercise.

I didn't know who Olivia Kelly was, but I made a mental note of the name. I wanted to know all Thayer's victims.

I was excited. Finally, I could tell Jim I knew, absolutely, who was bullying him. And more than that—I could offer him a way to fight back. Once again, I got to school early enough to corner Jim alone in homeroom.

"I don't cheat," he declared as I took the seat next to him. "I've never cheated in my whole life."

"I believe you," I assured him.

"Why would Paige say that?" he wondered.

"It wasn't Paige. It's Thayer Tillman. I can't tell you how I know, but it's true, I'm positive."

Jim was silent for a few seconds. Then he shrugged. "Oh, who cares. He's a jerk. He says stupid stuff all the time to everyone."

"He's worse than a jerk," I informed him. "He's a bully." I decided it was okay to offer more evidence if I didn't mention names. "He's been saying really awful stuff about a girl who wouldn't go out with him."

Jim frowned. "But why is he picking on me?"

"I don't know. Did you do something he didn't like?"

He seemed to be pondering this.

"I wonder if it has something to do with me replacing him as goalie, after he broke his foot saving that baby."

"That story isn't true," I said.

His eyebrows shot up. "He didn't break his foot?"

"Oh, he broke his foot, but it wasn't from jumping out of a house when it was on fire. He got hurt playing soccer with his cousin."

"How do you know that?"

"I just do."

I had a feeling that wouldn't be enough to convince him. I amended my comment.

"Well, I saw it happen." Which was actually true, in a way.

His mouth dropped open. "You mean, he made up that story about the fire?"

I nodded. "So this is my idea. Fight back! Tell people the truth! Make a poster and put it up in the school lobby. Let people know how Thayer really broke his foot. And they'll all start laughing at *him*! Even his own friends!"

"He'll be ghosted," Jim murmured.

I chose a better word. "Ostracized."

I waited for Jim to praise me for my idea and for giving him the ammunition for revenge. But he didn't. He shook his head.

"I don't think so, Kiara."

"Why not? You're on Nooz. You could post it everywhere."

"No, I wouldn't do that. Because then I'd be like Thayer. Turning people against someone. That's just not who I am."

What a nice person, I thought. Someone who would never want to hurt anyone else. Even if that anyone was hurting him. I wondered if I could be nice like that, and I thought about those kids back in elementary school who made fun of me. Even if I'd had ammunition, would I have done the same to them? Maybe. But probably not.

"Well, at least you could report him to the principal," I said. "I'm sure Mr. Lowell would do something."

But again, Jim shook his head. "First of all, I don't have proof that Thayer's the bully. Even if I *did* have proof and told Mr. Lowell, I'd be in even bigger trouble."

"Why?"

"Think about it. Thayer's a pretty popular guy. If he got punished, like suspended or something, his friends would all be after me. My life would just get worse."

I knew exactly what he meant, because this was exactly what happened to me. I was getting frustrated.

"There's got to be *some* way to stop him!" I cried out.

Jim almost smiled. "Well, if you come up with anything, let me know."

✦

At lunch, I told the others that Jim didn't want to use what we'd discovered about Thayer in the spyglass. Alyssa and Rachel had opposite reactions. Alyssa thought Jim was blowing off a good opportunity.

"He could really make Thayer look like a fool. I'd enjoy that."

I remembered the nasty way Thayer had spoken to her before, so I couldn't blame her. But Rachel seemed to understand Jim's feelings.

"Like Mami says, *No se puede combatir el fuego con fuego.* Then she translated. "You can't fight fire with fire."

✦

Later, at Ellie's, I was still thinking about Jim and wondering what he could do to stop the bullying.

"Jim won't report Thayer to Mr. Lowell either," I told the girls.

This time, both Alyssa and Rachel agreed with him. "Nobody likes a squealer," Alyssa declared.

A snitch, I thought, remembering what I'd been called. My friends were right.

"There was another person in Thayer's post today too," I told them. "Someone named Olivia.

That makes three victims. Jim, Paige, and this Olivia person. And maybe more. There are other social media apps, aren't there?"

"YouTube," Ellie said. "Back at my old school, kids put videos of each other on it. Of course, they weren't supposed to because they were underage, but they just lied about their birth dates and did anyway."

Rachel sighed. "I just don't know what Jim can do about this."

Ellie went to the spyglass. "Maybe this will give us an idea."

"See anything?" Alyssa asked her after a few seconds.

"Yeah. But it's got nothing to do with Jim."

We all gathered around her.

"What is it?" I asked.

"It's you," Ellie said.

My stomach turned over. "Like...that last time?"

"No." She moved the spyglass toward me. "Take a look."

I couldn't refuse. It would seem very strange. So I took the spyglass and peered into it.

It was a courtroom. And I spotted myself immediately. On trial, maybe. Accused of pushing that awful girl down the stairs. I shoved the spyglass away, and Rachel took my place.

"What does it mean?" she asked.

"Nothing!" I snapped. "I mean, there's that TV show I like, *Courthouse Chronicles*. I—I must be imagining myself on the show."

Alyssa took a peek. "It's fading," she said.

We went back to our beanbags.

"I still have a hard time thinking of Paige as a victim," Alyssa said.

"No kidding," Ellie agreed. "I thought I knew mean girls before, but she is positively the worst. And you know she won't want to do anything to support someone she calls a nerd."

Suddenly, out of nowhere, it hit me. That vision we'd just seen—it had nothing to do with *Courthouse Chronicles*. It wasn't about my fear, my memory of Chloe falling down the stairs, the other kids accusing me of pushing her. It had nothing to do with the past. It was the future.

I drew in my breath so sharply everyone could hear it, and they looked at me.

"What's the matter?" Ellie asked.

"Maybe Paige can help us," I told them. "She could be a witness."

They all looked at me blankly. I answered their question before they could ask it.

"We're going to put Thayer on trial."

twelve

"HAVE YOU EVER WATCHED *COURTHOUSE Chronicles*?" I asked.

None of them had, which wasn't surprising—it's not the kind of show that's popular with kids our age.

"Well, my father and I watch it every week, so I know a lot about how trials work."

"Wait a minute," Alyssa interrupted. "Don't people have to be arrested before they go on trial? Are we going to call the police about Thayer?"

"No," I said. "I'm talking about a mock trial."

"I know what that is." Ellie broke in. "My father

once told me about the mock trials they had when he was in law school, to practice for real trials."

"Yes, but this won't be any kind of practice. We're just going to act like it's a real trial, okay? We'll take on the roles of the participants."

They didn't seem particularly enthusiastic, and I wasn't sure they understood what I was saying, but I kept going anyway.

"First, we have to have a prosecutor, who's responsible for presenting the case, describing the crime, and proving that the person on trial is guilty. Then there's the defense attorney, who tries to prove that the person is not guilty. Or that maybe the person *did* the crime but isn't responsible because of some reason, like insanity or something."

"Thayer is bad," Rachel said, "but I don't think he's insane."

"Right," I said, "so that probably won't come up. Sometimes the judge shows leniency if the person has a good excuse. Like maybe the accused was really poor and had hungry children and stole a loaf of bread to feed them. Anyway, that's not relevant in this case. So, I want to be the prosecutor. Okay?"

Since, in my opinion, that was the coolest job, I was prepared for some competition. But no one objected.

"Who's going to defend Thayer?" Ellie wanted to know. "Not me!"

"Not me," Alyssa and Rachel echoed.

"Somebody has to," I said. "Even killers and drug dealers get lawyers. It's the law."

"If we're going by the law," Ellie said, "why don't we ask my father about this?"

Alyssa seemed to read my mind. "Let's not ask any parents to be part of this. They'll try to take over."

"Or tell us we can't do it at all," I added, thinking of my father's warnings about getting involved. "Anyway, the criminal chooses his own lawyer. Or the lawyer is provided by the court. We can figure that out later. Now we have to name a judge and decide on a jury and find a place to hold the trial."

"Wait a minute," Alyssa broke in. "How are we even going to get Thayer to agree to this? I mean, he has to be at his own trial, right?"

"This sounds awfully complicated," Rachel said. She got up and wandered over to the spyglass. "Let's look again."

"Wait a minute," I protested. "We're not finished. Let's talk about the jury."

But Rachel was already peering through the eyepiece and slowly moving the spyglass, and the others were looking at her.

"Anything there?" Alyssa asked.

"I don't know if it's a vision." Rachel turned the dial to magnify the image. "I see Mike. In the playground."

Alyssa looked at Ellie. Ellie shrugged.

"What's he doing?" she asked. "Looking at birds?"

"No, he's just sitting on a bench. Wait, someone's coming toward him. I can't see the face...oh, he's on crutches. It must be Thayer."

"Figures," Ellie muttered. "His best friend, the bully."

"Mike's looking at his phone," Rachel said. "He's shaking his head. Now he's showing the phone to Thayer. And Thayer's laughing." Then, a couple of seconds later, she said, "Wait, it's fading. I guess it *was* a vision."

"I've got it!" I yelped.

Rachel turned away from the spyglass. "You've got what?"

"Mike can be the defense attorney!"

Ellie was staring at me. She wasn't smiling. I explained my reasoning.

"Mike's a friend of Thayer's, so Thayer would trust him. But he's a friend of yours too."

"Was," Ellie corrected. "He *was* my friend."

"Well, you're just going to have to be friends with him again," I declared. "He's perfect for the job. And he'll be able to get Thayer to do this. Ellie, you need to ask Mike if he'll do this."

Now Ellie was glaring at me. "Haven't you forgotten something, Kiara? I'm not speaking to Mike."

I was beginning to feel frustrated, but I tried not to let it show. "Ellie, think of the greater good."

"Huh?"

"We want to make Thayer stop bullying people, right? That's important. And if you really care about that, you'll speak to Mike."

"She's right," Rachel said unexpectedly. "He *is* perfect for the job. I mean, it has to be someone who will be on Thayer's side."

Alyssa was nodding too. Ellie made a face and didn't say anything. But she seemed to be thinking, hard. Then she took out her phone and began composing a text.

Now that we were back on track, I continued with the plan. "As for the jury, it's usually made up of twelve people, but we can get by with less. Like six or eight. Rachel, you and Ellie can be on the jury."

"What about me?" Alyssa asked.

I shook my head. "Thayer called you a bad name, so you'd be biased."

"But we're all biased," Ellie pointed out. "We already know Thayer is guilty. We've seen him in the spyglass."

She had a point. "Okay, you're right. We'll have to ask other kids to be on the jury."

Rachel was clearly alarmed. "We have to talk to *them*?"

"Not the popular kids," I assured her. "We need jurors who don't know Thayer personally."

There was a moment of silence as we all tried to think of who those kids might be. Then Alyssa snapped her fingers.

"What about some eighth graders?" she asked. "They wouldn't know Thayer."

"Your sister's in the eighth grade, isn't she?" Ellie asked her.

"*Step*sister," Alyssa reminded her. "And forget it. No way I want her involved in anything I do."

"But we don't know any other eighth graders," Ellie argued.

Rachel spoke up. "I do."

"How?" Ellie asked. "And who?"

Rachel turned pink, which I knew meant that she was embarrassed.

"In September, I was having a lot of trouble in pre-algebra. I just couldn't get it. So Mom asked Mr.

Lowell if he would recommend a student who could tutor me. Kate Haskell's a math genius, and she was really nice too. She still says hello to me when I see her in the cafeteria at lunchtime."

Ellie considered this. "She probably knows some other brainy eighth graders too. It would be great to have some really intelligent people on the jury."

"That's good," I declared. "Okay, Rachel, you're in charge of getting us a jury. There's this thing they do on *Courthouse Chronicles,* where the lawyers on both sides question each prospective juror to see if that person is suitable."

Like I've said many times before, I'm not always great at reading expressions. But I couldn't miss the look of panic on Rachel's face.

"Well, I guess we can skip that part," I told her. "Just as long as they don't know Thayer, that's enough to make them eligible. But you have to tell Kate Haskell what we're doing and ask her to round up a jury for us."

Rachel bit her lower lip. Then, slowly, she nodded.

"Now we need a judge," I said. "Someone impartial. Maybe someone older than us. Someone who looks important."

"A teacher?" Rachel suggested.

"No, they'd probably know Thayer." I recalled

the expression they used on *Courthouse Chronicles*. "It would be a conflict of interest."

Alyssa grimaced and her brow was furrowed. I'd seen her do this before, several times, and by now I knew what it meant. She had an idea but she was reluctant to share it. I forced myself to look at her directly for once.

"What are you thinking?"

It seemed to take her a lot of effort, but finally she got out a word.

"Josh."

"Josh? Your stepbrother?" I asked.

Alyssa nodded. "He's seventeen. He's, like, a real high school big shot, he's president of the student body. And he's on the Honor Council there. When someone is accused of cheating, the Honor Council has a sort of trial thing to decide if the student's guilty."

I didn't understand. "But you didn't want your stepsister involved. Why is your stepbrother okay?"

"Josh isn't as horrible as Madison," Alyssa explained. "I mean, I don't *love* him," she added hastily. "But at least I can stand being in the same room with him. Barely."

I nodded. "Good, because he sounds perfect."

"Oh, he's Mister Perfect all right," Alyssa said.

I was puzzled. Alyssa had spoken before about her stepbrother, and she'd never said anything nice like that about him. Ellie must have seen my expression, because she grinned and turned to me.

"She's being sarcastic, Kiara."

Alyssa nodded. "But he'd be a good judge. And he won't know any of the other people involved."

I nodded. "Ask him."

Alyssa sighed. "For the greater good."

"Now, we need evidence," I said. "We can't use the spyglass. So we're going to need witnesses. People who will testify about experiencing Thayer's bullying."

"Jim!" Ellie said. Then she frowned. "But I think he might be embarrassed. Or worried that Thayer and his friends will make even more trouble for him."

"We have to talk him into testifying," I declared firmly. "What about Paige?"

"I really don't think she'll go along with it," Alyssa said. "It's like she said, he's in her clique. If she speaks out against him, the other kids in that group might get angry with her."

"But they already think she has a bad reputation," Rachel pointed out. "Maybe this is her chance to defend herself."

"Alyssa could be a witness," Ellie said. "Thayer said nasty stuff to her."

I shook my head. "But if her brother is the judge, I don't think she can be a witness. Conflict of interest. There's the girl Thayer said something nasty about in his last post. Olivia Kelly."

Ellie snapped her fingers. "I've got another one! Remember that sixth grader? The one Thayer tried to trip in the cafeteria?"

"Look for him tomorrow at school," I instructed her. "We want to have this trial as soon as possible before Thayer can hurt more people."

Just then, Ellie's phone made a message noise. She picked it up and looked at the screen.

"It's from Mike. He asked Thayer, and Thayer thought it was funny. He even wants to bring his friends to watch."

"But he'll appear?" I asked.

Ellie nodded. "And Mike will be his lawyer." Then she gasped. "That's what Rachel saw in the vision! Mike looking at the message, Thayer laughing...she saw the future! An actual event! Has that ever happened before?"

"Yes, it has," I said quickly, even though I wasn't sure. I didn't want them to get off the subject of the trial. There was another concern, and Rachel brought it up.

"Where can we have it?" she asked. "At school? Maybe in the auditorium?"

Ellie shook her head. "I doubt it. I think you can only have official school functions there."

"We'll think of something," I said. Then it hit me. "In fact, I've already got an idea."

thirteen

I MADE AN EFFORT TO RESOLVE THE LOCA-
tion of the trial at breakfast the next morning.

"Dad, I have a favor to ask."

"What's that?"

I chose my words carefully. "My friends and I,
we want to put on a...well, it's like a play. And we
need a place to perform it."

He waved his hand toward our large living room.
"That sounds nice. Why don't you do it here?"

"No, we need more space. There's a whole bunch
of people in the play. And we might have an audi-

ence. What we want is a big room, with lots of chairs."

"Can't you use a classroom at your school?" he asked. "Or maybe the auditorium?"

I thought quickly. "No, we're going to put the play on after school and the building will be locked." Actually, I didn't think this was true. I'd seen lots of notices, on walls and online, about after-school activities in the building. But my father probably wouldn't know about that. "Besides, it's not an official school thing," I added. "So they wouldn't let us do it at school. It's just me and some friends."

He looked at me in his usual "I'm concerned" way. "What friends? Ellie and the other two girls? Why do you need so much space?"

"Because I'm making more friends! And my friends have friends! Dad...I'm leading a normal thirteen-year-old's life here. Don't you think that's a good thing?"

His expression softened. "It is, honey. I just worry—"

I didn't let him finish. "My friends are great," I declared firmly. "I'm sure some people at school think I'm weird, but they don't call me names or anything." I added a little white lie. "I fit in just fine."

He smiled. "That's good to hear."

"So, can you think of a place where we can put on our play?"

I knew exactly what I wanted him to suggest, and he didn't fail me.

"There's a classroom next to my office that's empty on Thursdays from five o'clock on. I suppose you could use that."

"Great, that would be perfect!" I exclaimed. "Thanks, Dad."

He smiled. "Can I come and watch your play?"

I hadn't anticipated that request. Remembering how worried he'd been about my getting involved with bullying, I couldn't risk this. I thought rapidly.

"Um, no, I'm sorry, but I think my friends would be embarrassed if there was an adult in the room."

He seemed to accept that and nodded. "Of course, I'll be in my office next door. I hope *that's* okay."

As long as you stay there, I replied silently. I felt pretty good about this. I hadn't told any really big bad lies. We were all playing roles, so a mock trial *was* kind of like a play.

◆

As we'd agreed, the sisterhood met at school before homeroom, and I told them that we now had a space for the trial. Alyssa told us that her stepbrother had agreed to serve as judge. It was all good—but they weren't too happy when I told them we would be going to trial on Thursday.

"That's just three days from now!" Alyssa yelped. "We have to find a jury, talk to witnesses..."

"We can do it," I declared. "I'll talk to Jim in homeroom. We have to find out who this Olivia Kelly is and talk to her."

"That's easy," Ellie said. "She's in our English class."

"She is?" I shouldn't have been surprised. I never paid any attention when Ms. Gonzalez called on people other than me. "Okay. Rachel, you're going to talk to Kate Haskell at lunch."

Rachel looked faintly sick, but she nodded.

I went on. "Ellie, talk to Mike, and tell him Thayer has to take this seriously."

Ellie frowned. "I'm not sure I'm ready for an actual conversation with Mike."

"Well, *get* ready and do it today!"

Ellie frowned. "You're getting awfully bossy, Kiara."

Which is usually your job, I wanted to say, but somehow I managed to hold it back. I'd been working hard on not saying everything that was in my head, and I was improving.

"I'd better go in and catch Jim before the bell rings," I said, and left my friends. When I got into the room, I went over to Jim, and didn't waste time with greetings and salutations.

"Are you angry about being bullied?"

"Sure."

"You want to do something about it? Because I've got a real plan."

I told him about the trial, and I didn't have to coax or beg or argue with him. He immediately agreed to be a witness.

Later, I raced to English class to get there before the bell. Alyssa was already there, and she pointed out Olivia Kelly to me. Ellie and Rachel came early too, and we approached Olivia together.

"Are you on Nooz?" I asked her.

"Yes," she said, "and before you ask, I saw the post." Then, to my surprise, she grinned.

"You're not upset?" Rachel asked.

"Why should I care what some jerk says about me? I don't even know who the Champ is."

"It's Thayer Tillman," I told her.

She laughed. "That figures. He's a *major* jerk."

"You're right," Ellie agreed. "But he's got some kids really unhappy."

Olivia's smile faded. "Yeah, like Jim Berger, I'll bet. Thayer just called me names and made a dumb threat that he'll never carry out. He told real lies about Jim."

"We're putting Thayer on trial," I told her.

And Olivia Kelly agreed to be a witness too.

✦

We had another success at lunch. Ellie spotted the sixth grader that Thayer had tried to trip in the cafeteria a couple of months ago. As Alyssa and I got on line to get our lunches, Ellie took off after him.

When we emerged with our trays, we joined Ellie and Rachel at our usual table and Ellie gave us a thumbs-up.

"The sixth grader's name is Tom Dillard. He skipped a grade in elementary school, he's like some kind of genius and he's just ten years old. He said Thayer's made fun of him before in the cafeteria. Like, asking him if he'd escaped from kindergarten, that sort of thing. And really loud, of course, so everyone could hear. Now, what about our jury? Have we got that set up?"

I looked pointedly at Rachel, who shifted around in her seat and wouldn't look at me.

"Come on, Rachel," I said, "you talked to people when you were campaigning to be seventh-grade representative."

"I know," she replied. "But I didn't like doing it."

"I'll go with you," Ellie offered.

I wasn't crazy about the way Ellie was acting, like she was in charge. But on the other hand, I certainly didn't want to go talk to strangers. So I said nothing as Ellie and Rachel got up and walked to the back of the cafeteria, which was known as eighth-grade territory.

There was someone else we had to contact. I looked around the room.

"There's Paige," I announced. I looked at Alyssa.

"No way I'm going to ask her in front of her friends," Alyssa said. "I'll send her a text."

"Do you think she'll agree to appear as a witness?"

Alyssa seemed to be considering that. Then she grinned. "I was with her in the second grade when she wet her pants in class. I could threaten to post that online."

I made a face. "That's not nice. But maybe for the greater good..."

"I'm kidding!" Alyssa exclaimed. "Kiara, you never get my jokes."

Because I didn't think they were funny. I didn't say it, though.

Rachel and Ellie returned to the table. "We've got a jury!" Ellie proclaimed happily. "Kate Haskell and five other eighth graders."

✦

At Ellie's that afternoon, I was feeling pretty good. Things were really falling into place. Alyssa had texted Paige, and she hadn't received a response, but with the three others confirmed I thought we were okay. I felt a huge weight fall off my shoulders. It was going to happen. Suddenly, I felt something else, an enormous range of feelings that I couldn't identify. This must have shown on my face, because the others were all looking at me.

This made me uncomfortable, so I had to turn away from them. I got up and went to the spyglass. As I peered through the eyepiece, I spotted something right away and magnified it.

"What do you see?" Rachel asked.

"Thayer."

"Real or vision?" Ellie asked.

I wasn't sure at first, and then I realized he wasn't on crutches so it was a vision.

Thayer was alone in the park and making a pile of rocks. Then, as a person walked by, Thayer tossed a rock at him. Two girls came along, and he said something I couldn't hear, but it made them run away. Then he went up to some little kids who were throwing a ball back and forth. He grabbed the ball and threw it up into a tree. The children started crying. And there was a big grin on Thayer's face. I knew he was laughing at the people he was hurting. And maybe at the idea of going on trial.

I remembered what the prosecutor on TV said.

"We gotta nail this guy."

fourteen

ON WEDNESDAY EVENING, I JOINED MY FATHER in the living room to watch *Courthouse Chronicles*. I brought a notebook and a pen, and I sat on the floor so I could use the coffee table as a desk.

"What are you doing?" Dad asked.

"I want to take some notes. For the trial tomorrow. I mean, for the play about a trial."

"Don't you have a script?"

"Well, it's actually kind of a…a…" I *knew* the word, but I had to think hard to come up with it. "An improvisation," I declared triumphantly. "We make up the lines as we go along."

"Oh, I see." He picked up the remote and pointed it toward the TV.

First came the opening scene, which showed the crime. There was a guy working on a computer, and it soon became apparent that he was hacking into places where he shouldn't be. Then the bad stuff happens: a college kid gets a notice telling him he's failed some big exam. He gets really upset, to the point where his roommates actually call an ambulance and the boy is hospitalized. His parents come rushing to the hospital to see him. Then they learn that the notice was a mistake, possibly caused by the hacker, and the boy didn't fail the exam. But the whole hospital business has cost his family so much money that he can't go back to the expensive college. The parents tell the police, and the police find the hacker and arrest him.

Next came the theme music of the show and pictures of the regular cast. Then there was a commercial, and after that, the trial began.

I didn't pay much attention to the actual proceedings. I just wanted to get down some of the special words and phrases the lawyers and the judge were using. Quickly, I scribbled *All rise, I call to the stand,*

You may proceed, No further questions, Your Honor.
I was writing so furiously, I wasn't really paying attention to the proceedings.

I was determined to make tomorrow's event seem like a real trial. The image of Thayer laughing in the spyglass vision was still making me angry. Maybe using these legal expressions would make him realize this was serious business.

Then there was the closing music and the credits were rolling on the screen. Dad turned to me.

"Well, what did you think?" he asked. "Good trial?"

"Um, I'm not sure. What did *you* think?"

He cocked his head to one side, which meant he was thinking.

"Well, the prosecution didn't have much of a case. The defense put that psychiatrist on the stand who testified that the boy had emotional problems before this happened, and that he was prone to deep depressions. The prosecution couldn't actually prove that the exam failure had caused his breakdown."

"So the hacker wasn't guilty," I said.

"Weren't you listening, Kiara? The jury found him guilty!"

"Oh! I guess I was thinking about something else. Why did they find him guilty if the prosecution didn't make the case?"

"I think it was the defendant's attitude."

Since it was difficult for me to judge someone's attitude, and my father knew this, he wasn't surprised when I asked him to explain.

"The hacker was very arrogant," Dad said. "Practically bragging about his expertise. He condescended to the jury."

Condescended. . . . Once again I had to search my mental dictionary. "He was acting like they were beneath him?"

I could tell my father was pleased that I understood. "Exactly! He made it clear that he didn't think they were intelligent enough to understand him or judge him. You know, a jury could have all the facts, but if the defendant isn't likable, that can affect their decision."

This was good to know. Thayer Tillman certainly wasn't a very likable guy. I couldn't understand why people like Thayer and Paige were so popular. Maybe I just don't understand *popularity*.

I closed my notebook. "I'm sleepy," I declared. "Good night, Dad."

I wasn't really tired. My mind was racing so fast that I didn't know how I'd ever get to sleep that night.

I ran over everything I'd done to see if there was anything I still had to take care of. Everyone—Mike, Thayer, the jury members, the witnesses—had been notified as to the time and place tomorrow. A couple of the witnesses had asked if they could bring friends to watch, and I'd given them permission. On the TV show, there were always observers in the courtroom. And Ellie had told me she'd put a note in the mailbox of the *Eastside News,* the school newspaper. Maybe there would actually be something interesting to read in the next edition.

I couldn't think of anything else I needed to do, but I still wasn't ready to go to sleep. So I picked up *A Wrinkle in Time* and opened it to where I'd left off.

I was almost finished with the book. I didn't have to write a report on it, but Ms. Gonzalez had said we'd each have to say something in class about our books—what they were about and what we thought about them.

I couldn't say I'd *loved* this book. Some of the fantasy characters seemed sort of silly to me. But the real people, they were okay.

In my head, I went over what I might say about it. The book is about how Meg Murry, her brother, and a friend travel to another planet to free her dad, who's a scientist, from evil forces. To get to him, they have to go through something called a tesseract, which is a real scientific thing, but in this book it's described as a wrinkle in time and space, which doesn't really exist. I liked this part.

The father was on a planet controlled by something called IT, which was evil, but Meg was able to defeat IT with love. So she rescued her father and saved the planet from this evil power.

Personally, the idea of love as a weapon didn't appeal to me as much as a laser or some sort of stun gun. But it was still interesting. And I kind of identified with Meg. She was very smart, but she didn't have many friends and she felt like an outsider. She was different, and at the beginning of the book she wished she could be more like her normal classmates at school. I could relate to that.

But love... could love fight evil? I thought about the struggle I was having to stop Thayer. I wouldn't call him evil, but he was definitely not good and maybe was hateful. At least, that was how he behaved. Could I use love as a weapon? What did I love?

Then the answer came to me. Justice. I loved justice. That had to be why I loved *Courthouse Chron-*

icles. And maybe why I hadn't liked *The Crucible* very much, because justice wasn't applied.

Justice could stop people from doing bad things. And that was what I was trying to do. I wouldn't save a planet, like Meg. But maybe I could make East Lakeside Middle School a nicer place.

fifteen

ON THURSDAY AFTERNOON, AT HALF PAST four, my father opened a door and beckoned for Ellie, Rachel, and me to enter.

"Will this work for you?" he asked.

"It's perfect!" Ellie exclaimed.

I agreed. This particular classroom at Bascomb College had seats for around thirty people. I didn't think we'd get that big an audience, but at least the room wasn't so large that it would look empty if there were just a few observers. There was a large wooden desk at the front, which would serve for the judge.

I was also pleased to note the way Dad was looking at my friends. He wasn't acting alarmed or concerned—in fact, he was actually smiling. He approved of them! I was kind of hoping he'd leave and go back to his office next door before Alyssa arrived. She wasn't always all that friendly, she could even be rude sometimes, and I wasn't sure how he'd react to that or to her goth look, which some people found disturbing.

"Go ahead and rearrange chairs as you like," Dad told us. "Just make sure it's back the way it is now when you're finished."

"We will," Rachel told him. "And thank you for letting us use the room, Mr. Douglas."

Just then, a boy appeared at the open door. "Are you still doing office hours now, Dr. Douglas?"

"Yes, Mark, go on in, I'll be right there."

Rachel's face had turned completely pink. I knew this meant she was embarrassed.

"I'm sorry!" she exclaimed. "I should have said thank you, *Dr.* Douglas."

My father smiled. "That's quite all right, my dear. Now I'd better go speak to my student. Good luck with your play, girls, and I'll be right next door if you need me."

Once he'd left, I took over. "Okay, we need to make this look like a courtroom." Conjuring up memories of *Courthouse Chronicles,* I began pulling a chair over to the side of the desk.

"This is the witness box, where each witness will sit. We have to move six chairs against the wall for the jury. Two chairs in the front row on that side for the lawyer and the defendant, one chair on the opposite side for me. And we need a chair in front of the desk for the court reporter."

"Who's that?" Rachel asked.

"Alyssa. She can type the fastest and she's bringing her laptop." Another idea hit me. "And she can be the person who swears in each witness."

"Wait a minute," Ellie interrupted. "You said she couldn't be on the jury because her stepbrother is going to be the judge. How can she have those jobs? Isn't that a conflict of interest?"

She was probably right, but I wasn't going to admit it. Ellie always acts like the boss of the Spyglass Sisterhood, which, again, I suppose is natural since she has the spyglass. But this time, *I* was in charge, and I was about to remind her of that when Alyssa ran into the room.

"You're not going to believe this!" she cried out. "Josh bailed on us!"

I stared at her in disbelief. "He's not going to be our judge?"

"He hurt his ankle playing basketball this afternoon and he had to go to the doctor. He claimed he was in agony." She then performed one of her eye rolls, which I knew meant she didn't believe it. "What are we going to do? The jury and the witnesses and everyone else will be here any minute!"

"We'll have to ask someone else to act as judge," Ellie said.

"Like who?" Alyssa asked. "At least Josh knew something about judging from being on his Honor Council. I don't know anyone else who knows anything about trials except Kiara, and she's the prosecutor."

My mind had been spinning like a wheel since Alyssa's announcement, and it finally settled on a name. It wasn't the most appealing notion, and something I would have rejected if anyone else had suggested it. But we were desperate, and as I once heard a lawyer on *Courthouse Chronicles* say, desperate times call for desperate measures.

"Wait here," I told them. I left the room. Just as I approached the next door on the hallway, it opened and my father's student came out.

"Thank you, Dr. Douglas," he was saying.

I heard Dad respond. "You're welcome, Mark. Please close the door behind you."

I ducked in before Mark could do that.

"Dad, I have another favor to ask."

He glanced up from his computer screen. "Just a second, Kiara, I have to put a note in Mark's file."

While he did that, I looked around the room. I'd never actually been in my father's office before, but it looked pretty much like his study at home. Books on shelves covered the walls. There was one item that was unfamiliar. Hanging from a coatrack was a long shiny black robe with gold stripes on the sleeves.

Dad must have noticed what had caught my attention.

"That's the gown I wore when I received my PhD. Now I wear it here for our graduation ceremonies. All the professors wear their gowns at commencement, and each gown is different, because each represents the college the professor attended. It makes for a nice procession when we march into the auditorium."

I supposed that was kind of interesting, but I had more important things on my mind. "Okay. Listen, Dad, this play we're doing, it's about a trial. And the person who was supposed to be the judge can't come, he's sick. Can you play the judge?"

"But I don't know the lines," he protested.

"You can wing it, Dad! I told you, it's an improvisation. You watch *Courthouse Chronicles*, you know what judges say. *Objection overruled! Call the next witness!* Please, Dad, we're desperate!"

He seemed to be considering it. "You know, Kiara, I've served on juries in real trials. Twice."

"So you're an authority!" I pointed out.

He smiled. "All right, I'll do it."

"Great, thanks, Dad. I'll come and knock on your door when we're ready for you."

I hurried out and went back to the classroom. Some people had already arrived. In the back of the room, Mike was sitting with Thayer and some other boys I recognized from their lunch table. I hoped they wouldn't start yelling stuff or making jokes. But then my father could say "Order in the court!" And since I knew what my father looked like when he was angry, I figured that would shut them up.

When I told the sisterhood about our new judge, Ellie frowned. "I thought you said we weren't going to let any parents get involved."

I was expecting this, and I'd prepared a response. "You have a better idea?" I challenged her.

She didn't. So I moved on to give Alyssa the sheet of instructions I'd prepared for her and then went to the back of the room to see Mike. Ignoring Thayer, I handed Mike a sheet of paper.

"Here's my list of witnesses."

He handed me his list, and I gave him another paper.

"And these are the instructions for the defense counsel," I told him.

He glanced at the paper and handed it back. "I already know this stuff, Kiara."

I was skeptical. "How?"

"I watch *Courthouse Chronicles.*"

And here I thought I was the only person at our school who watched that show! Now I had someone else to discuss it with. But not right at this moment.

Glancing at Mike's list, I saw three names. Jackson Blair—the name sounded familiar, and I thought he might be in one of my classes. The second was Amir Khan, and that didn't ring a bell at all. The third was Thayer himself, and I was pleased. I could bring up his lie about the fire and saving the baby and show the jury what a jerk he was.

I saw Rachel greeting Kate Haskell and the others who I assumed were eighth graders. Rachel sent them all to sit in the jury area.

The next to arrive was Jim Berger. He looked a little pale, but he walked in quickly and came directly to me. From the back of the room, Thayer yelled, "It's the nerd king!" Jim didn't flinch, but given the situation, I thought he must be nervous, so I spoke in the gentlest tone I could muster.

"You okay?"

"Yeah, I'm fine."

"I'm calling you as the first witness," I told him, and led him to a seat just behind mine. Another witness, Olivia Kelly, arrived, and I seated her next to Jim. Then I checked both names off my list. Looking up, I saw a small boy I didn't recognize at the door. Someone's little brother?

"Who's that?" I asked Ellie.

"Tom Dillard. The ten-year-old sixth grader Thayer picks on."

"Really? He looks even younger than that."

I noted his age by his name on my list. The fact that he was younger than the average middle grade student might make him more sympathetic to the jury.

"Show him where to sit," I told her, and she did. I was pleased that she was accepting my leadership. I had to admit, I was enjoying this.

There was still one witness missing. I had a sinking feeling that Paige might not show up. Alyssa had never received an answer to the text she sent Paige. Watching the door, I noticed another boy I didn't recognize walking in. I went up to him.

"Who are you?" I asked

"Steve Wong, *Eastside News*. And who are you?"

"Kiara Douglas. I'm the prosecutor."

He opened the notebook he was carrying. "Can you spell your first name for me?"

I did, and he wrote it down. Was I actually going to get my name in the school newspaper? I wasn't sure how I felt about that. But I couldn't think about it now, so I just pointed to the rear of the room. "The press is in the back." At least, that's where they always sit on *Courthouse Chronicles*.

Still no Paige. I thought I had enough evidence to convict Thayer without her, but I'd be sorry if she didn't show up. I might not understand her popularity, but I know that popular kids get lots of attention.

I went to my seat, opened the backpack I'd left there, and took out the gavel I'd brought for Alyssa's stepbrother, which would now be for my father. It wasn't a real gavel. I'd found it ages ago in a store where you could get holiday gifts on sale when the holidays were long past, and I'd planned to give it to my father on the next Father's Day. There were words on it: HAPPY FATHER'S DAY on the handle and DAD'S IN CHARGE! on the round part, which actually made sense in this situation. But you couldn't see the words from a distance, and it looked like a real gavel, though it wasn't as heavy as I thought a real gavel would be.

I was just about ready to summon my father when Paige appeared. I couldn't read her expression—it wasn't happy or sad or angry, just one of those looks I can never figure out. Alyssa showed her to her seat with the other witnesses, Ellie and Rachel joined the jurors, and I went to get my father.

I rapped on his office door. "Dad? We're ready for you."

"I'm coming," he called.

I went back into the classroom-courtroom and nodded at Alyssa. She looked at her instruction sheet.

"All rise!" she yelled.

"Why?" Thayer yelled back. But Mike elbowed him, and Thayer stood along with everyone else.

Dad came in. At least, the man who entered was definitely my father. But at that moment in time, he was someone I didn't know at all. And it wasn't just because of the long black graduation robe he'd put on. His face was set in an expression I didn't think I'd ever seen—very, very serious. He had to walk right past me, but he didn't glance at me and smile or wink. He looked straight ahead as he strode toward the desk and stood behind it.

Alyssa checked her paper again. "Court is now in session," she read. "Judge Edward James Douglas, PhD, presiding."

Dad sat down, picked up the gavel, and hit the desk. It only made a tiny tapping sound, but the room was pretty quiet now, so it could be heard.

"You may be seated," he declared, and we all sat down. He looked at the sheet I'd placed on his desk. "The court will now hear the case of the People versus Thayer Tillman."

Those friends of Thayer's, sitting in the back, started laughing, and so did Thayer. My dad picked up the gavel again, but then he put it down, made a fist, and pounded the desk twice. *That* made real noise.

"Order in the court!" he commanded.

The room went silent. I glanced at Thayer. He looked surprised, and he'd stopped laughing.

"Are all parties present?" Dad-the-judge asked. I had to start thinking of him as just the judge. I was afraid I might slip and call him Dad.

I stood up, just like the prosecutor on TV always does. "Kiara Douglas for the prosecution, Your Honor."

And then Mike rose. "Mike Twersky for the defense, Your Honor."

My father nodded. "The prosecution may make its opening statement."

I'd committed this to memory. "Your Honor, members of the jury, the People accuse the defendant, Thayer Tillman, of committing acts of bullying toward students at East Lakeside Middle School. The prosecution will demonstrate how his actions have caused harm to these students."

"You may call your first witness," the judge said.

"The prosecution calls Jim Berger," I announced.

Jim got up and I pointed to the witness chair. Alyssa jumped up from her place and read aloud.

"Please raise your right hand. Do you swear that the testimony you are about to give is the truth, the whole truth, and nothing but the truth?"

"I do."

I moved so that I was directly facing him.

"Jim Berger, do you go to East Lakeside Middle School?"

"Yes."

"What grade are you in?"

"Seventh."

"Do you know Thayer Tillman?"

"Yes."

"Has Thayer Tillman bullied you?"

"Yes."

"When did the bullying start?"

"Well, I don't think he's ever liked me. I mean, he

sometimes called me names like Shorty or Skinny. But I guess he started the actual bullying a few weeks ago."

"Please explain how the bullying took place."

He shifted around in his seat, and I didn't think he was just trying to get comfortable. Was he chickening out? I wondered. But finally, he spoke.

"He started posting comments about me on Nooz. He made fun of how I played soccer. He told other people to pick on me. He wrote that I cheated on tests. And some of his friends started making comments to me that weren't nice."

Jim took a deep breath and started blinking rapidly. I had a feeling he was trying not to show how he was feeling. I just hoped he wouldn't start crying. Personally, I wouldn't mind, because it would make the jury have more sympathy for him. I'd seen on *Courthouse Chronicle*s how juries reacted when someone cried. But I'd also heard that boys get incredibly embarrassed if they cry in public. And I didn't want to make it worse for Jim.

"The worst thing was, he told lies about my family. He posted a picture of my father talking to a police officer in a parking lot, and he said my father was being arrested."

"How did this affect you?"

Jim pressed his lips together tightly. Then he paused, as if he was thinking about this.

"Well, kids were looking and pointing at me, and laughing. Some people asked me if my father was in jail. It was all pretty embarrassing."

"Thank you. No further questions."

"Does the defense wish to question this witness?" the judge asked.

Mike rose. "Yes, Your Honor." I stepped aside and he took my place in front of Jim.

"You said the person who bullied you posted mean comments on Nooz. How were these posts signed?" Mike asked.

"The Champ," Jim replied.

"And how do you know that the Champ is my client, Thayer Tillman?"

I hadn't expected this, and I looked at Jim anxiously. He glanced in my direction and then responded to the question.

"Someone told me. A classmate."

"And how did that classmate know this?"

"Um, I don't know. But I believed her...him... this classmate."

"Did this classmate show you any proof that the Champ is Thayer Tillman?"

"No."

"No further questions."

"Would the prosecution like to redirect?" the judge asked. It must have occurred to Dad that not everyone watched *Courthouse Chronicles,* so he explained to the room.

"This means that the prosecution can now ask questions to counter what the defense has asked the witness."

I was very annoyed with myself. Why hadn't I guessed that Mike would bring up the fact that we couldn't prove the Champ was Thayer? I could have prepared something. But I hadn't, so I didn't have anything to say.

"No, Your Honor."

"Then you may call the next witness."

"The prosecution calls Olivia Kelly to the stand."

Olivia was sworn in, and I began with the same questions about who she was. Then I asked if Thayer Tillman bullied her.

She didn't hesitate. "Yes, he called me a fat, ugly pig on Nooz. And he said he was going to chase me home from school so I could get some exercise."

"And how did this make you feel?"

She grinned. "I laughed."

That was not what I wanted to hear. "Didn't it hurt your feelings?"

"No." She shook her head, just once, but decisively. "Because I'm not a fat, ugly pig. I'm a big, beautiful young woman."

She was right, but this wasn't good for my argument.

I persisted. "But didn't you feel threatened, that he was really going to chase you home?"

"Not really. He's a stupid jerk, but he was just picking on me. I didn't think he'd really do it."

"But you didn't know that for sure, did you?"

She shrugged. "I guess not."

I should have told her beforehand to say she was afraid. But if she wasn't afraid, she'd be lying, and she was under oath. I gave up.

"No further questions, Your Honor."

"Redirect?" the judge asked.

"How was the post signed?" Mike asked, standing again.

"The Champ."

"And how do you know the Champ is Thayer Tillman?"

Again, she shrugged. "Someone told me. And It sounded like him. I mean, it's the kind of thing he would say."

"But did Thayer Tillman ever say this to you in person?"

"No."

"No further questions, Your Honor."

This was not going well, I thought. I glanced at the jury, but of course, being me, I couldn't read anything in their expressions. But one girl had her eyes closed—not a good sign. And one of the boys was looking at his phone! Were they bored? I couldn't be sure. But this trial had to get more lively.

At least the next witness had actually *seen* his bully.

"The prosecution calls Tom Dillard."

The little sixth grader looked scared, even I could see that. I smiled at him, but that didn't seem to help. He kept glancing at Thayer. I turned and saw that Thayer was making an ugly face at him. I stepped a little to the left in the hope that I'd block Tom's view of him.

"How old are you, Tom?" I asked.

"Ten," he mumbled.

"And you're in the sixth grade?"

"Yes."

"Have you been bullied?"

He swallowed, and then he nodded. "I guess. Yeah."

"How?"

"Someone called me Pipsqueak. And asked me if

I was lost and looking for my mother. It was a girl, and I don't know her name."

This wasn't what I wanted to hear. "What else?"

He mumbled something.

"Could you speak up?" I asked.

"I...was tripped in the cafeteria. Well, someone tried to."

"Can you identify the person who tried to trip you?"

I stepped back to the right to give him a clear view of the defendant. With a shaky hand, he pointed.

"Let the record show that the witness has identified Thayer Tillman," I declared. "Has Thayer Tillman bullied you in other ways?"

Looking at the floor, Tom nodded, and recounted remarks Thayer had called out to him in the cafeteria. Like, had he escaped from kindergarten. And did the drinks machine carry baby bottles.

"He asked me where Snow White was. Like I was one of the Seven Dwarfs. And if I was the one called Dopey. And he said all this stuff really loud, so people around him were laughing."

When it was Mike's turn, he offered Tom a bigger smile than I'd been able to muster up.

"When you were tripped in the cafeteria, were you injured?"

"No."

"Why not?"

"Someone grabbed me before I could fall." Tom's eyes widened in recognition. "Hey, I think it was you!"

"Objection, Your Honor!" I called out. "This isn't relevant."

I could have sworn Dad almost smiled. "Objection sustained. Jury will disregard that last statement."

"Is it possible that this was all an accident?" Mike asked. "That Thayer didn't mean to trip you?"

Tom frowned. "I heard you tell him to cut it out."

Mike turned to the judge. "Objection, Your Honor. My presence at the event has already been declared irrelevant."

My father actually smiled. I wondered if maybe he was impressed with Mike's lawyer talk.

"Objection sustained. Jury will disregard that statement."

Now I was getting really worried. My case was becoming dependent on that awful Paige Nakamura. When I called her to the stand, I was relieved when she looked past me and glared at Thayer.

Paige was sworn in by Alyssa, and then she sat down. Her expression was so grim that I had no problem identifying it. She was angry. This was promising.

After establishing her identity, I began with the usual question. "Have you been bullied at school?"

"Yes." She pointed, and her arm wasn't shaking at all. "Thayer bullied me."

She was getting ahead of herself, but that was okay. I quickly reordered my line of questioning.

"How did Thayer bully you?"

She proceeded to tell the story of what happened when he asked her to go to the movies. "So when I said I couldn't, he started posting nasty stuff about me on Instagram. On Snapchat too. And he started spreading rumors about me to my friends."

"Did your friends believe what he said?" I asked.

"Some of them did," she admitted. "The thing is, I'm pretty popular at school, so there are always going to be people who are jealous of me."

I ignored that. "What kind of rumors did he spread?"

"Like, that I wanted to hook up with *him,* and *he* was the one who rejected *me.* As if I couldn't do better than Thayer Tillman!"

"And how do you know that your bully is Thayer Tillman?"

"My friends told me what he was saying. And I knew he liked to call himself the Champ since he won the bowling tournament. In the *fifth* grade." She emphasized *fifth* as if to point out how old his claim to fame was.

"And how did this bullying affect you?"

"It hurt my reputation!"

This was *good*. "No further questions, Your Honor."

It was Mike's turn.

"Do you still have those Instagram texts on your cell phone?" he asked.

"No, I deleted them," Paige replied.

"How about the posts on Snapchat?"

She looked at Mike as if he was stupid. "Snapchat posts only last for a day."

"So you have no real evidence of the bullying?" he asked.

"My friends know about it."

"Are they here to testify on your behalf?"

She pressed her lips together tightly, and I guessed what might have happened. She'd asked them, but they'd said no. Either because they were loyal to Thayer, or maybe testifying at a trial wasn't considered cool enough for them.

"No."

"No further questions."

Mike took his seat, and the judge turned to me.

"Do you have another witness to call?"

I thought about whether there was anything else I could do. I couldn't think of anything.

"No, Your Honor," I said. "The prosecution rests."

sixteen

"CAN I GO NOW?" PAIGE ASKED ME.

"No, I might need you for rebuttal."

"For *what*?"

Obviously, Paige had never watched *Courthouse Chronicles*.

"I'm just saying you can't go till it's over," I snapped.

She took a step backward. I figured she was stunned that a nobody like me would dare to give orders to a popular girl. Although, to be honest, I didn't feel like a nobody that day. But I wasn't feeling great either. Mike was doing really well, and I was not looking forward to seeing what he was going to do with his defense of Thayer.

"The defense may present its first witness," the judge declared, and Mike stood up.

"The defense calls Jackson Blair."

One of Thayer's friends, a really tall boy with close-cropped hair, came forward. Alyssa recited the oath, and the boy sat down on the witness chair.

"How long have you known Thayer Tillman?" Mike asked.

"Since third grade."

"What kind of person is he?"

Jackson shrugged. "He's cool. Fun."

"Have you ever witnessed him bullying anyone?"

"Nah."

Mike turned to the judge. "No further questions, Your Honor."

I got up and approached.

"Do you know Paige Nakamura?"

"Sure, who doesn't?"

Even though I couldn't see her, I could imagine Paige preening behind me.

"What kind of person is she?"

Jackson shrugged again. "I don't know. Okay, I guess." Then he glanced in Thayer's direction and amended that. "But she's not as cool as she thinks she is."

"What did you think of Thayer's comments about her on Instagram and Snapchat?"

Mike jumped up. "Objection, Your Honor. There's no proof that my client posted anything on Instagram and Snapchat."

"Objection sustained," the judge said.

I felt a sudden urge to scowl at my father, but I resisted it. He wasn't my father here, and he was supposed to be impartial. Frantically, I tried to recall what the lawyers always said when their questions were thrown out. Then I remembered.

"I'll rephrase. Did you see comments about Paige on social media?"

"No."

"You're under oath," I said sternly.

He reconsidered. "Yeah, maybe."

"What did you think of those posts?"

He shrugged again. "I don't know."

I tried again. "Did you think the comments were nasty?"

I hoped the jury caught the brief smile that crossed his face.

"Yeah, a little," he said. "But she deserved it."

"Why?" I asked.

"Well, she disrespected him."

"Meant nothing to me!" Thayer yelled.

The judge pounded on the desk. "Order in the court! Mr. Twersky, please tell your client he can't interrupt testimony."

Dad's voice was louder, so I thought he was irritated, but I was excited.

"So you're saying that Thayer Tillman *was* responsible for the social media posts!"

"I didn't say that!" Jackson protested.

It was my turn to smile. "No further questions."

Mike then called Amir Khan to the witness stand. Another boy rose, and then I recognized him. He was one of the guys who was always at the cafeteria table with Mike and Thayer.

Mike asked Amir pretty much the same questions he'd asked Jackson—how long he'd known Thayer and did he think Thayer was a bully—and he received pretty much the same answers. Then it was my turn.

"Were you with Thayer Tillman when he tripped Tom Dillard in the cafeteria?" I asked.

"It was an accident," Amir said calmly. "The sixth grader didn't see Thayer's leg stretched out."

Amir was a lot smoother than Jackson, I realized. He wasn't going to be so easily rattled.

I nodded. "Were you with Thayer Tillman when

he *accidentally* almost tripped Tom Dillard in the cafeteria?"

"Yes."

"And you're absolutely, positively sure it was an accident?" I asked. "Remember, you're under oath."

He paused. Then he replied, "That was how it appeared to me."

Aha, I thought. *He's honorable, and he isn't going to lie under oath.* And I knew where to go next.

"Did you see posts about Jim Berger on Nooz?"

"Yes."

"Do you know who wrote those posts?"

Amir's expression changed. I wasn't sure if he was suddenly worried, or scared, or what. His eyes moved away from me, in the direction where Thayer was sitting.

"I'm not sure," he said finally.

"Is it possible that Thayer Tillman wrote those posts?"

There was another pause. And then he said, "Well, I guess anything's possible."

It was the best I'd get out of him, but it wasn't bad. I still needed someone to come right out and confirm Alyssa's statement that Thayer was the Champ.

"No further questions." I went back to my seat, and Mike got up.

"The defense calls Thayer Tillman."

Thayer had to use his crutches, but even limping he looked totally in control. I glanced at the jury, and I thought I could maybe interpret some expressions. A boy's eyes narrowed, and he was shaking his head slightly as he watched Thayer make his way to the stand. One girl had her nose wrinkled, like she smelled something bad. And I was pretty sure there was no odor in the room.

On *Courthouse Chronicles,* the judge always reprimands the jury if they show any reactions. I guess Dad didn't notice. His eyes were on the accused.

Thayer started to sit down on the witness chair, but Alyssa stopped him.

"You have to stand to take the oath," she declared. "Put up your right hand."

I could see him wink and grin at Mike and his witness-friends in the front row, and I wondered if he even heard the words she was saying. Not that it mattered. I didn't think he was like Amir—Thayer would probably lie under any circumstance.

Mike asked his first question. "Thayer, do you think you're a bully?"

"No," Thayer said loudly.

"Can you describe what real bullies do?"

It was clear to me that Mike had practiced these

questions with Thayer, because Thayer spoke as if he'd memorized the answer.

"Bullies are people who order other people around and make the people do what the bullies want them to do."

"Can you give me an example of a bully?" Mike asked.

Again, Thayer responded quickly. "Sure. I saw a movie about a bully. He was making people give him money so he wouldn't hurt them."

"Would you ever do something like that?"

"No way. I don't have to ask people for money." He grinned. "Except my parents."

That got a little laugh.

"If you're not a bully, why do you think you're on trial here?"

"Because some people can't take a joke," Thayer replied.

"No further questions." Mike walked back to his chair and Thayer stood up. But then the judge spoke.

"You have to answer questions from the prosecution, young man."

Thayer scowled and sat back down. I came over and stood a little closer to him than I'd done with the other witnesses. I was hoping that would make him uncomfortable. Sure enough, Thayer fidgeted in his seat.

"Is a bully someone who picks on other people?" I asked.

"Depends," he said.

I took a deep breath. I absolutely had to ask the next question in the right way if there was any chance of getting the answer I wanted.

"When you posted those comments about Jim Berger on Nooz, were you picking on him?"

"I was just teasing!" he snapped.

I raised my voice. "So you admit that you posted those comments! You're the Champ."

He stared at me, his mouth open, but no words came out.

The judge spoke. "The witness will answer the question."

Thayer looked in the direction where Mike and his witnesses were sitting. But of course, they couldn't help him.

"I'll repeat the question," I said. "Do you admit that you wrote the comments about Jim Berger and posted them on Nooz?"

Finally, Thayer spoke. "I don't remember."

At that point, to show what a liar he was, I'd

planned to ask him how he broke his foot. But then I thought better of it. Lying about being a hero didn't make him a bully, and Mike would object to the question.

"Did you try to trip Tom Dillard in the cafeteria?" I asked.

"That was an accident," Thayer replied.

"And what about threatening to chase Olivia Kelly home?"

"That was a joke!"

I smiled. "So you did post *that* comment on Nooz, too?"

Once again, I'd rendered him speechless. I glanced toward the jury to make sure they were getting the significance of this.

"And what about Paige Nakamura? Did you post mean things online about her too?"

He was getting angry, I could tell. And I was glad. When people get mad, they don't think about what they're saying.

"Paige Nakamura is a total—" He caught himself just in time. Instead, he finished with "—a liar. She's a total liar."

"So you didn't ask her to go to the movies?"

"Yeah, I asked her, so what?"

"And she refused to go with you."

"Yeah, so what?" he said again.

"But then you told everyone that she asked *you,* and that she was actively seeking a boyfriend. That she was even going after someone else's boy-friend, and—"

He didn't even let me finish.

"I was *teasing*!"

I smiled again, glanced at the jury again, and then said, "No further questions."

"The witness may step down," the judge said.

Thayer reached for his crutches, but Mike jumped up. "Your Honor, may I ask my client a few more questions?"

I looked at the judge and saw my father. I had an easier time reading him than other people, and I could see an expression I recognized. He was wor-ried, and suddenly I knew that he'd figured this whole thing out—it wasn't a play. It was real life.

He nodded. "I'll allow it. You may redirect."

Mike approached Thayer.

"Thayer, I'd like to ask you some questions about your family," he said.

"Objection!" I called out. "Relevance?"

"I'll show why this question is important, Your Honor, if you'll give me some...some..."

I knew he was trying to remember the word they

used on TV and I knew I shouldn't help him out, but I couldn't resist.

"Latitude," I whispered.

"Some latitude," Mike repeated.

"All right, you may proceed."

"Thayer, do you have an older brother?"

"You know I do!" Thayer said.

"Tell the court his name and age."

Thayer shrugged. "Carson. He's sixteen."

"How do you and Carson get along?"

"Okay, I guess."

"Does Carson tease you?"

"Yeah, sometimes. I mean, that's what brothers do, right? I tease him too."

"Does he order you around?"

Thayer gave a short laugh. "He tries to."

"And what happens when you don't do what he says?"

Thayer didn't answer.

"Does he get physical?" Mike asked.

"Huh?"

"Push you? Hit you?"

Thayer shrugged.

"Answer the question," the judge ordered.

"Not really," Thayer said. "I mean, we horse around, you know?"

"He's bigger than you are, isn't he?" Mike asked.

"Yeah, sure, he's older."

"So he could actually hurt you when you horse around."

I could barely hear him when he muttered, "Yeah."

"What do your parents do about this?"

"Nothing."

"Nothing? Not even when Carson hurts you?"

"He doesn't mean to!" Thayer declared. "He—he doesn't know how strong he is."

"Your parents don't criticize him?" Mike asked.

Thayer shrugged. "Carson's their favorite. Like, he makes really good grades. He's got a learner's permit for driving, so when my mother doesn't want to drive, he takes her places. And he shoots hoops with my father on the carport."

"You don't shoot hoops with your father?"

Thayer's voice was barely audible. "He says I'm crummy at basketball. My game is soccer."

"Does he compliment you on your soccer playing?"

Thayer shrugged again. Mike didn't press him for an answer.

"Does your mother compliment you about anything?"

"She doesn't pay any attention to me. Except to criticize me."

"What about your father? Does he hit you?"

"No. He just yells a lot."

"What does he say?"

Thayer shifted around in his seat. He was uncomfortable.

"You know," he said to Mike. "You've been in my house."

"Does he call you a big nothing? Does he tell you you're worthless? Is he constantly threatening to ground you?"

I knew I could object at this point. Mike was putting words in the witness's mouth. But I didn't. I wanted to hear Thayer's answer.

"Yeah."

Mike nodded. "Are you bullied at home, Thayer?"

This time, Thayer's mumble was inaudible. But he nodded slightly, so I knew the answer.

Mike paused, took a deep breath, and said, "That's all I have to say. The defense rests."

"Does the prosecution want to redirect?" the judge asked.

What could I ask? Thayer's testimony had shaken me up. I shook my head. "No, Your Honor."

Thayer left the witness stand. It was now time

for closing arguments. I had mine written down, and I read it out loud. It was just a rehash of the evidence—how Thayer made fun of people, hurt them, told lies about them.

"Thayer is a bully," I concluded. "He should be punished for what he's done, and he should be stopped from doing it anymore."

Then Mike rose and addressed the jury. "You've heard a lot of bad things about Thayer. Maybe some of them are true. But there are reasons he's like this. What lawyers call mitigating circumstances." He shot me a look and we almost exchanged smiles. Then he continued.

"Thayer isn't treated well at home. He feels like a victim. So when he's at school, he tries to be powerful. And sometimes he treats other people the way he's treated at home. It's—it's not really his fault. He doesn't know better."

I looked at Thayer. His face was beet red, he was clenching his teeth, and his hands were curled into fists. Mike had to be seeing this too.

I looked at the judge and saw my father looking very sad.

"The case will now go to the jury," he said.

seventeen

IT WAS VERY QUIET IN THE ROOM AFTER THE
jury left. Dad had sent them to his office for their
deliberations, and most of the people left in the
courtroom had taken out their cell phones to check
messages or play games. What surprised me was
seeing the judge take out *his* phone and look at it.
Dad pretty much only ever used his phone to take
and make calls, so I didn't know why he even both-
ered to have a smartphone.

As for me, I was just trying to understand how
I was feeling. I thought I should be feeling trium-

phant. After all, I'd made Thayer admit to what he'd done. And Thayer had done some really awful things. In my opinion, he was a bad guy. But according to Mike, there was a reason for this. Did that make Thayer less bad?

I didn't have much time to contemplate this. The eighth graders returned in ten minutes. They walked single file to their places, not giggling or whispering or poking each other. I wondered if we would be like that in a year. They seemed so cool and confident, like they knew what they were doing. It was hard to believe that one year could make that much of a difference in style.

The judge raised his eyes. "Ladies and gentlemen of the jury, have you reached a verdict?"

Kate Haskell stood up. "We have, Your Honor."

"In the case of the People versus Thayer Tillman, on the sole count of bullying students, how do you find the defendant? Guilty or not guilty?"

Kate spoke loudly and clearly. "We find the defendant guilty."

"Ha ha, very funny." That came from Thayer. He rose unsteadily on his crutches. "You're all a bunch of losers. C'mon, guys, let's get out of here."

But none of his friends budged. And from his desk, the judge spoke firmly.

"Stay where you are, young man. I have not pro-
nounced your sentence."

Thayer snorted. "This isn't a real trial. What are
you going to do? Lock me up? You're not even a real
judge!"

"No, I can't lock you up," the judge said. "I
don't *want* to lock you up. You should be punished
for what you've done, though. But first, I want to
explain why."

There was something about his voice that made
everyone sit up and pay attention.

"I'm not an expert on bullying, but I've had some
experience with it. And I'm not a psychologist, so I
can't say I understand why some people bully. But
while the jury was out, I took a look at some recent
articles on bullying by authorities on the subject."

So that was why he'd been looking at his phone.
His eyes swept the room. He was talking to everyone, not just to Thayer.

"I know that bullying has become an epidemic
among young people, particularly in middle schools.
This is antisocial behavior, and it's very danger-
ous. The victims may suffer academically. They
may lose self-esteem, become depressed. They may
even harm themselves. And the bullies suffer too.
Research shows that bullies are more prone to sub-

stance abuse, and they are more likely to commit criminal acts."

Now he turned his attention to Thayer.

"Mr. Tillman, you spread rumors about Paige Nakamura, a classmate who rejected you. You mocked Tom Dillard, a student in the cafeteria who was younger than you. You threatened Ms. Kelly. You posted untrue stories about Jim Berger. You intended to harm these people. Maybe not physically, but definitely emotionally."

Dad paused, as if to let this sink in. Then he continued.

"I understand that there are problems which may have caused you to behave like this, and these problems need to be addressed too. For the sake of your victims, and for *your* sake, this behavior has to end."

Now Thayer was staring at the floor. I didn't know how he was feeling, but I was pretty sure it wasn't good.

"Thayer Tillman, you have been found guilty of bullying, and I will now pronounce your sentence. Tomorrow morning, you will report to the school principal and confess to your crimes. He will determine your punishment."

Thayer looked up. "And what if I don't?"

The judge gazed at him steadily. "You may have

noticed that you are surrounded by classmates who have witnessed this evening's trial. I feel fairly confident that word of this will get back to your principal whether you tell him or not. Also, I believe there is a reporter present, am I correct?"

That boy from the school newspaper in the back of the room stood up.

"That's me."

"And do you plan to report on this trial?"

"You bet! I mean, yes, sir."

"Well, be careful. There were personal stories that emerged in the testimony that the subjects may not want to be made public. Consult with them before you print anything."

"Yes, sir, I will."

The judge turned back to Thayer. "Getting back to my original point, I think it's in your best interests to see the principal yourself, Mr. Tillman. Before he hears about this from others."

Thayer slumped down in his seat.

Dad-the-judge pounded the table with his fist.

"This court is adjourned."

eighteen

MS. CAVENDISH HAD PREPARED A FEAST FRI-
day evening.

"It's about time there were some folks here!" she
declared as she put another plate of little sandwiches
on the table next to the punch bowl.

I gave her my version of Alyssa's eye roll. "*We're*
folks, Ms. Cavendish. You, Dad, and me. So is Aunt
Molly, and she comes here a lot."

"I'm talking about a *party,*" she said happily, and
went back into the kitchen to check on her cheese
sticks.

I'd never given a party before. And besides the birthday parties I went to as a little kid, the only one I was ever invited to was the grand opening of Aunt Molly's salon. Since I hadn't known anyone there except my father and my aunt, I spent that entire party on one of the salon chairs that gave you a massage when you pressed a button.

I knew everyone who was coming tonight. The party was actually my father's idea. He said it would be an opportunity to celebrate our win at the trial. But I think he really wanted a chance to get to know my friends.

The sisterhood girls were the first to arrive, and Ellie had news for me.

"Just before I left home, I looked in the spyglass and saw you!"

"Getting pointed at again?" I asked.

"No. You were walking down a hallway at school and actually talking to people. And some of them were shaking your hand! And clapping you on the back!"

I flinched. "Hitting me?"

Alyssa did an eye roll. "It's a way of congratulating people, Kiara."

Actually, I had to admit, I *liked* that vision. Not that I thought I would suddenly become the queen of East Lakeside Middle School, but this was a good indication that I was no longer a nobody.

Mike came next, with Jim Berger.

"You must be feeling pretty good," I said to Jim.

"A lot better," he admitted. "But I feel sorry for Thayer."

I was astounded. "Why?"

"Because he's had a rough life, and maybe he doesn't really want to be a bully. I just hope he gets some help."

He was right, I thought. I'd spent so much time thinking of Thayer as the enemy, I'd forgotten he was a human being. And human beings could change. *I'd* changed. On the other hand, Paige Nakamura would probably never change.

Ellie and Mike stared at each other for a few seconds. Then Ellie put out her hand, Mike shook it, and I figured that meant they were friends again. Or at least, not enemies.

Kate Haskell arrived, with Steve Wong, the reporter from the school newspaper, and one of the other jury members, Brian something. I really had to start learning people's names.

Ellie had given me some tips about appropriate party behavior, so as my guests arrived, I led them over to my father and Aunt Molly so I could introduce them. There was another knock on the door and I went to answer it. It was Olivia Kelly with someone I hadn't expected—Amir Khan.

"I know I was on the other side," he said to me. "But Olivia thought it might be okay if I came with her."

"It's okay," I said. "You were pretty good on the witness stand."

"I was trying not to lie, but not to hurt Thayer at the same time," he told me. "You guys were right, you know. I mean, Thayer's my friend but he can do some really stupid stuff."

I understood. "Mike Twersky's here, and he's Thayer's friend too."

Mike was right behind me. "Not anymore," he said. "At least, not for a while. He hates that I told people about his family." He sighed. "I was just trying to drum up some sympathy for him. I mean, having a crummy family situation doesn't excuse the way he behaved, but maybe it shows he's not naturally mean. I hope he can change."

Rachel and Alyssa joined us. "Did you invite Paige?" Rachel asked me.

"Yeah. She said she didn't go to parties like this one."

Alyssa did her eye roll. "You mean, with people like us?"

Mike laughed. "Some people never change."

"I wonder if Thayer can change," I said. "Did he go to see the principal?"

Amir nodded. "He was suspended. Mr. Lowell called his parents in, and he told them Thayer could come back in a week if all of them saw a counselor together. That whole family needs help."

Steve the reporter came over and caught the last words. "We might get some real help with this bullying stuff. We're doing a big piece in the paper about it, how the schools have to develop a program to deal with bullying, make it part of the curriculum and all. Thayer's not the only bully at East Lakeside."

"That's good news," Mike said.

"And we owe it all to Kiara," Alyssa declared. She raised her glass of punch. "Here's to Kiara!" she said loudly.

Everyone in the room turned toward me and raised their glasses. "To Kiara," they called out in unison. I could see Aunt Molly beaming, and my father—he was smiling, but he also looked like he was about to cry.

Steve shook my hand and Mike clapped me on the back. Ellie sidled up next to me. "See? It's just like my vision!"

"What vision?" Mike asked.

Alyssa shot Ellie a fierce look, and Ellie flinched. "Uh, it was a dream I had."

All this attention was making me a little uncomfortable. Fortunately, people began to move around. Some went to the table where Ms. Cavendish had placed an enormous chocolate cake. The boys drew closer and started talking about the soccer team. I overheard Kate Haskell telling Aunt Molly that she was bored with her hairstyle, and Aunt Molly telling her to stop by the salon.

I went over to my father. He knew I didn't really like crowds and people looking at me, so he was probably concerned.

"Everything okay?" he asked.

"Sure," I replied. I figured that wouldn't be enough to convince him, so I added, "I'm just not used to this."

"I know," he said. "It's all pretty new for you. Being a leader. Having friends."

For one brief moment, I thought about my old life. Alone with my computer screen—I'd always felt so safe there, so comfortable. Nothing could hurt me.

"It's a little scary," I admitted.

"Understandable," he said. "But you can handle it."

I nodded as if I agreed, but inside I was thinking, *Maybe.*

Dad moved closer to me. "I'm very proud of you, Kiara."

He put an arm around my shoulders and hugged me. And for once, I let him.